TRIALS AND REDEMPTION

THE STORY OF RAY WILLIAMS:
THE RELUCTANT OUTLAW
A Christian Western

ALLEN LINN

Minneapolis, Minnesota
patrickday@pyramidpublishers.com

Printed by Lightning Source
1246 Heil Quaker Blvd. La Vergne, TN USA 37086
ISBN – 978-1-7351068-4-7
Unless otherwise noted, Scripture quotations are from The Holy Bible, New International Version®, NIV®. Copyright © 1973, 1978, 1984, 2011 by Biblica, Inc.™ Used by permission of Zondervan.

Cover Design by Alexander Galutsky
Interior Design by Pyramid Publishers
Printed in the United States of America

1

Ray Williams grew up in a small town in Abilene Texas. His parents, Bob and Sarah, worked hard turning their plot of land into a self-sustaining ranch, starting with a few head of cattle and some chickens and a good sized garden. Ray grew up knowing a hard life. As a youth he was stricken with scarlet fever and had been rather frail growing up. But as a teen, hard work had turned him into a strong hardworking young man. He was a loving and obedient son.

He felt a special concern for his parents who nursed him through his very contagious illness. During that time he could see their love for him that he never forgot. Their own safety was always secondary to his. They both worked very hard but were never too busy to spend time with him. They read to him stories from the Bible which had a great influence on his life. He was devoted to making his parents lives as good as possible.

The territory he lived in was very violent and had many outlaws; so along with the work on the farm, his dad spent time showing him how to handle a gun. First he taught him what a gun was not for. He was never to look for trouble and was to realize that a gun, though necessary in these parts, was always to be used as the last resort. His father's guidelines were not always easy to follow, especially in a territory like this, with young, foolish and proud toughs strutting around wanting to show how fast they were with a gun. It was especially stressful on days Ray had to go into town, about three miles away, and get supplies. But even at 18 Ray was good at minding his own business.

Ray was taught that killing a man was nothing to be proud of and backing down from a senseless gunfight was nothing to be ashamed of. A gun was always to be used for good. His dad would often quote their minister or one of the circuit riders that covered this territory. These circuit riders were very appreciated by most everyone. This was a tough territory, and these were tough men who were devoted to their job. The life expectancy of a circuit rider was short. They would ride to their assignment, do their job of preaching for three or four days, receive their meals and a place to sleep from grateful people, but then would roll up their sleeves and go and chop wood or do some other work for their keep. They persevered through freezing cold, extreme heat, and sickness. They had no permanent home but depended on the hospitality of others, many of whom were antagonistic and hostile toward them. Many times, they were pelted with rocks and garbage.

Nothing kept them from fulfilling their assignments. They would go to disease-stricken areas and preach the gospel. They were not afraid of death because they had given their lives to Christ to do His will. To be a circuit rider they had to be "sold out" to God. They truly earned their respect. By the time of his eighteenth year, Ray had acquired a good knowledge of the Scriptures.

Along with the hard work on the ranch, Ray and his father would hunt and tend the garden. His parents taught him the Bible. They agreed with America's founding fathers that no education was complete without learning the Bible. The founding fathers were educated in the Scriptures and their political writings were filled with Biblical quotations and allusions because the early colonists were biblically literate and lovers of the Bible. This is what enabled them to establish the greatest nation in history.

Ray learned to read mostly from the Bible, and his parents taught him math and writing. Between this education and his practicing at shooting and his work of farming and hunting and his attending church services, he had a full and satisfying life.

One day when he turned twelve years old, a circuit rider gave him a biography of George Washington and reading it made an indelible impression on him. Washington's strong faith in God and providence (God's leading and guidance and provisions) gave him an unshakable assurance that God was aiding the fledgling new country and gave him great courage to engage in daring moves that completely surprised the enemy during the war with England. He ordered his soldiers not to use profanity or gamble or abuse alcohol or show inhumanity to the enemy, so as not to alienate God's superintending care over their just fight for freedom.

He never sought fame. Congress pleaded with him to lead the Continental forces against the British in America's war of independence, which he did without financial compensation. He displayed his heroism and unshakable faith in God as he endured with his troops the hardship of the terrible winter at Valley Forge.

After six years of war, aided by the French fleet, Washington forced the surrender of the British forces at the battle of Yorktown. Again, Congress pleaded with him that only he could lead in the beginning of the new nation. He was unanimously elected the first President of the United States. After four years, he was told that it was vital that he served a second term as President. After eight years he retired from public service at the age of 64.

He saw the threat to liberty of the people becoming

dependent on one man, the very thing he had dedicated his life to fight against. His refusal to serve more than two terms was for the good of the nation. He always put principle above personal gain. If the experiment of constitutional democracy were to succeed, he would have to back away and pass the torch to others.

On September 17, 1796, he announced his farewell from public life. From this moment on, the survival of American freedom would no longer depend on him but on the character of its people and the government they would elect. His final message to the American people was: "Of all the dispositions and habits which lead to political prosperity, religion and morality were indispensable supports: "It is impossible to govern rightly without God and the Bible."

When Washington was sworn in as President, he chose to have his hand on the Bible, a tradition that would continue with following presidents. At the conclusion of his inauguration he bent down and kissed the Bible; then he led those in attendance across the street for a two-hour worship service to commit the new nation into the hands of God. It was important as the first president to set a standard for following presidents.

Ray would often go into deep thought on why he was here. Was there a purpose for his life? Did God watch over his life like He did over George Washington's life?

His parents were determined that he would have what they did not have. His mother was raised in a loving Christian home, but Bob, his dad, lost his mother when he was seven years old. His father became bitter toward God and turned to alcohol. For the next eight years, Bob learned to live with an abusive, drunken father who truly loved him but was helpless to give him the care he needed, until his father was brought to Christ by a Circuit

Rider.

After that Bob's father was a changed man. By then his father's health had been broken and he lived only two years after that, during which time Bob cared for him. He held no grudge for the years his father neglected him but thanked God for the first-hand knowledge that God had given him of the power of the gospel to change a man's life. He had seen many who claimed to be Christians but showed no evidence of it and it made him wonder if God was real. He wished he could talk to George Washington rather than read about him. In books, many things happened that never seemed to happen in real life. He often wondered if God were real. His father's conversion was God's answer.

At seventeen, Ray's father married Sarah, through whom he learned the influence of a godly upbringing, and a year later Ray's older brother Morgan was born. They lived in the cabin that his father had built before alcohol got a hold of him. Three years later Ray was born.

Ray's older brother, Morgan, lived on the other side of town with his wife and two children. There was an Indian tribe in the area but the Williams and the other homesteaders in the area got along with them, but still they were protected by a garrison of troops stationed about ten miles away.

Though they did not understand each other's language very well, they did pick up enough words to understand each other along with some sign language to stay on friendly terms. Once two braves helped pull one of their cows out of a ditch, and now and then, in the winter, the Williams would give a beef to an unsuccessful hunting party of Indian braves. However they were not always friendly.

The settlers always had to be on their guard. Sometimes some of the riffraff in town would get drunk and ride out and hassle the Indians. Once they raped and killed a young Indian girl. For a long time there was tension between the Indians and the white man. Luckily the Williams had built up a respected reputation with the Indians. Many whites considered Indians inferior and sub-human, but anyone who had close contact with them knew better and they could learn a few things about character and bravery from them.

Ray developed a very healthy respect which, after a while, turned to love for them. Once when he was twelve years old, while hunting with his dad, they were separated from each other and Ray, unknowingly, went onto Indian land where he shot a deer but before it hit the ground an arrow found its mark. He suddenly realized that he had entered Indian land. Two very tall, powerful looking Indian braves stood looking down at him and the deer. Ray was terrified and threw down his gun and held his hands up.

They appeared majestic to Ray. He was both afraid and impressed by these powerfully built men. They laughed and one patted Ray on the shoulder and pointed at the bullet hole and by some kind of sign language, that Ray finally grasped, was telling him that the deer was his. Many times Ray had heard how savage Indians were and this incident made an impression on him that he never forgot.

Ray insisted that they take the deer. They were impressed with his honesty and sincerity. After studying him for a moment one of them pulled out a large knife and put a gash in the palm of his hand and pointed at Ray's right hand. Ray knew he meant to cut his hand. He had a fear of having his hand cut but the sense of honor he felt made the pain insignificant and he desperately wanted to impress them with his bravery. He held out his hand and allowed him to put a small gash in his hand. The expression on his face and the tears in his eyes made them both smile as he pressed his palm against Ray's, mingling their blood.

The Brave went to a certain bush and reached up and grabbed some healing leaves and took some in his own bleeding hand and held them and closed his hand around them and put some in Ray's hand and Ray closed his hand around them. Ray knew something very significant had just taken place and couldn't wait to tell his father. He clearly felt a definite kinship with these men.

He ran back to his father and told him what had happened and showed him his hand. Bob frowned, greatly concerned, examining his hand, he said, "You be careful son. I told you not to go on their land."

"I didn't mean to, I didn't know," he said. His father could see that Ray was disappointed by his father's mild rebuke.

"I'm happy for you son, you should be proud, but remember, not all Indians are friendly toward white men. They have not been treated very well by them. So always be cautious, accept their friendship and be willing to help them, but be very careful. They can be very good friends or fierce enemies."

After a week of hard work, on s Saturday. Ray's dad hitched the horse up to the wagon and called for Ray to go the three miles to town with him for supplies. They were going to meet Morgan in town that day. Morgan and his wife, Rachel, and their two children lived about a mile up the other side of town. Sarah's birthday was coming up and Morgan wanted Bob's help to find a gift for her. Sometimes Ray's dad and brother would have a beer at the saloon while Ray gathered the needed supplies.

That day there were many cowhands passing through town, who had been working on a cattle drive,. Their work was done for a while now that the cattle had been delivered to their destination, and today was payday and they would wash the dust down at the bar. This was always a time for the sheriff and his deputies to be on the alert.

When Bob saw Morgan, he stopped the wagon and jumped down and went with Morgan. They visited a store that sold dresses while Ray took the wagon and got the needed supplies and loaded them on the wagon. After about an hour, Bob and Morgan decided on a blue dress for Sarah's birthday. They had the dress gift wrapped and walked over to the saloon for one quick beer.

After buying and loading the supplies on the wagon, Ray walked over to the dress shop. He did not find them there and walked over to the saloon where Bob and Morgan were. As he stepped onto the walkway, a cowhand staggered out the door and rudely shoved Ray out of the way. Ray backed up a step and bumped into another cowhand behind him, heading for the saloon. Both men laughed at him and rudely motioned for him to get out of the way.

Just then, Bob and Morgan came out the door as the two men went in. "Just in time," Ray smiled at them. The two cowhands came back out the door. "Did you say something?" one of them said with a sneer, obviously looking for trouble. "He wasn't talking to you," Bob said curtly. The cowhands glared at him in drunken stupors.

As Ray, Bob, and Morgan walked down the street to their horse and wagon, they noticed the cowhands following them at a short distance with angry looks on their faces. Just then, they were met by the Sheriff and two deputies, "that's right boys just ride away," the Sheriff said. Bob nodded to him. A moment later, the cowhands were stopped by the sheriff and his deputies, "Hold on, you guys are going to wait here until they ride away," the Sheriff said.

"You have no right to hold us here," one of them said while poking his finger into the sheriff's chest. His deputies grabbed him. "I'm afraid you three are going to do a little time in jail," the sheriff said.

"For what? on what charge?" asked a tall lanky cowhand with his eyes bulging out along with the veins in his neck.

"To keep the peace. Or, if you insist, for assaulting a peace officer!" the sheriff said, rubbing his chest in mock pain where the cowhand had poked him with his finger.

As Ray, Bob, and Morgan rode off, the sheriff waved and they heard the angry curses and threats from the cowhands, which they ignored. Little did they realize how deadly this little dispute would turn out.

Later that day, five men visited Ray and his parents. As they rode up to the fence, Bob was in the garden and Ray and Sarah were in their cabin. No one knew what to expect; they were not expecting anybody. The men dismounted from their horses while Ray watched from the window. One of the men came through the gate carrying a lantern. When he got close enough to the house, he flung the lantern through the window. Ray recognized him as one of the cowhands from town. When it hit the wall it threw flames everywhere as the oil splattered throughout the house. Ray grabbed his gun and fired through the window, hitting the cowhand in the neck. Ray couldn't believe this was happening; it was more like a dream.

Two of the other men walked toward Bob, firing their guns several times before Ray shot one of them, hitting him in the temple, but a third man hit Bob in the shoulder. Bob dropped his gun as he fell. As he crawled toward his gun, another bullet tore through the side of his chest just under the armpit. Ray came out of the cabin shooting and killing the man. The other two men rode away, but Ray got a good look at them.

Ray got Sarah out of the burning cabin to safety and then ran to his dad. His dad stared at him with horror in his eyes. Ray could see that he wouldn't last long. He knelt down to comfort his father. Ray knew what his dad's fear was. "We're both all right," he said as Sarah walked toward them.

His dad pulled Ray's head down and gasped into his ear, "You take care of your mother and yourself."

Ray felt a terrible dread as he felt his dad's hands go limp and his eyes closed for the last time. He ran to his mother and pulled her toward the barn. She struggled and pulled free and ran the other way, toward Bob. Ray followed her. She held Bob's head in her arms and kissed him, "We have to go, there's nothing we can do for him now," Ray said sobbing and pulling her away.

She collapsed beside her husband. Ray ran around to the barn for the horse and wagon. He came back and helped her on the wagon and drove the four miles to his brother Morgan's ranch. Morgan and his wife, Rachel, came out and they helped Sarah off the wagon and into the house. Inside, Ray explained what happened. His mother was clearly in shock. After getting her settled, he rode back to town to report the incident to the sheriff. He found out from a deputy that the sheriff had gone out to the cabin after the two men who got away had reported that they had gone out to make amends and were fired upon. Three of their friends were killed, and they claimed that they had had no choice but to kill his father in self-defense.

Ray was stunned and rode back to Morgan's place and discussed what to do. They decided that he would leave his mother with Morgan, and Ray would run for it rather than answer questions about the killings. He would get a job at a nearby ranch and send Morgan money to help care for his mother. A friend of Morgan's recommended a rancher he knew who needed to hire a man. Ray rode out to talk to the owner of the Wagon Wheel Ranch in Sherman Texas, and got the job. It was about ten miles away, a little further than he wanted but it would do nicely. A couple times a month, he'd ride to Morgan's ranch and give him some money to help out.

He stayed at Morgan's place until after his dad's funeral. He spent some time with Reverend Mills who conducted the funeral before he left. The minister assured him that his dad was a true believer in Christ. Ray said he wanted to know why God allowed this to happen. The reverend told him that we live in a fallen world and bad things happen to good people. God wants us to trust Him in the dark. God doesn't always give us answers, but he does give us many promises that He is in control and will make everything right to those who love Him.

The Wagon Wheel Ranch was spread over 1600 acres and employed 16 men supervised by a stocky built foreman named Tom Hansen. Ray's job was to go each day where he was needed as a kind of handy man. Some days he would break horses, other days he would help in the kitchen or feed the livestock or mend a fence, or if one of the steady hands were sick, he would fill in for him that day. Ray liked the variety of Jobs rather than the monotony of the same job day after day.

Now and then, the hired hands would have to guard against rustlers and thieves and disputes with other ranchers. So it was pretty common to find a hired gunman or two to protect their rights. The Wagon Wheel Ranch outdid all the others when they hired Jack Garth to settle all disputes.

Garth had been in and out of jail since he was fourteen years old. His parents were both killed in a shootout with lawmen just before his fourteenth birthday. After that he was on his own doing odd jobs for his room and board. He practiced with a gun constantly until a rancher hired him to protect the interest of their ranch. Soon he became well known for his fast gun, and ranchers began to pay him top dollar for protection. All of the other hired Guns feared him and he knew it. He relished the fear he struck in the hearts of men, including those on the Wagon Wheel Ranch. He had a cruel streak. No one really liked him but they all feared him and that's all he cared about.

Ray started his job on the Wagon Wheel Ranch with two others repairing fences. There were stray dogs in the area looking for food. Ray would always put food aside at suppertime and bring it out for them while working. Ray loved dogs, and it bothered him that Jack Garth would take potshots at them. So Ray always made sure to feed them when Garth wasn't around. The evenings were spent playing horseshows or poker. Sunday was their day off but they had to be back at camp by dark. Ray would attend church and spend time reading his Bible.

The work was hard, the food was good, and the pay was fair. Ray's mind was always on his mother at his brother's ranch. He missed his dad and some nights he would sit out on the porch alone and cry. It eased him of much tension. His mind was still confused at how fast his life had changed.

He made friends with another hand named Logan Nash. He learned that Nash wanted to be a Texas Ranger, but hard times made it necessary for him to hook up with some desperate men who taught him how to survive, including by theft when necessary. He was Ray's age, about twenty. They became good friends and worked together for the next three months.

It was irritating to see Jack Garth strut around with a superior look on his face. Ray especially didn't like the way Garth treated the cook, an old man named Jim Hayes. He would degrade him mercilessly if any of the food was not to his liking. Ray desperately wanted to avoid trouble with him, but he could sense that things were headed that way, so Ray avoided him as much as possible. Ray and Logan did their jobs and steered clear of Garth. They avoided him at all costs. Ray just wanted to be left alone and earn money to send to his mother.

After three months Ray's mother died. She never fully recovered from that terrible night his dad was murdered. He attended her funeral and Logan insisted on going with. Again, Ray wanted to know why. Again the reverend said he could not tell him why, but he could tell him that Christ loved him enough to die for him and God was asking Ray to trust Him. "Well, He asks a lot from a person!" Ray shot back.

The reverend put his arm around Ray. "He knows that son, He asked a lot of Himself when He gave His only begotten Son to die on a cruel cross for our sins. Anyone can trust when things are going good, but God wants a genuine trust in Him when things are going bad," the Reverend said.

"You make a lot of sense reverend, but it's still hard," Ray said.

"Someday we will be able to understand, but until then God wants us to trust Him" the reverend said.

After attending her funeral and riding back with Logan to the Wagon Wheel Ranch one Sunday, the inevitable happened. Garth shot one of the stray dogs just for the fun of it. This was the breaking point for Ray. After all the suffering and misery he had seen recently, this senseless killing and the glee on Gath's face was the final straw. Ray's eyes met Garth's for several moments. He knew he was asking for trouble but he could not hide the contempt he felt. Garth would not tolerate what he considered disrespect, but Ray was at the point where he just didn't care anymore.

Garth glared at him and turned and went into the bunkhouse. Ray knew he had stirred up a hornet's nest. Ray figured that his days were numbered after today, if he made it through the day. Ray grimly buried the dog then went into the kitchen for supper. Eating was impossible. He just sat at the table contemplating going in to the bunkhouse. He had mixed emotions of fear and anger. Finally it came down to simply not caring what happened to him anymore, if it meant a clash with Garth so be it.

He didn't find being alive such a big deal anyway!

When Ray went into the bunkhouse, it was ominously empty except for Jack Garth, who sat at the table quietly drinking whiskey. Again their eyes met; neither man could hide his dislike for the other. The only difference was that Ray felt a genuine fear, even a dread of the man who sat at the table in front of him. He had to go past him to his bunk in the other room. He took a deep breath and walked toward his bunk trying not to show his fear. Garth drew his leg up and planted the bottom of his fancy boot against a beam blocking Ray's path.

Ray stopped suddenly trying to keep his legs from shaking. Garth's lip curled in a half sneer and half smile. He was clearly enjoying himself. His eyes bore into Rays like steel daggers. Ray felt a cold chill run through his body. His heart was pounding uncontrollably. His throat was dry. His breath came in short gasps.

Garth grinned gleefully at the fear that Ray could not hide. "I have a way of making men realize their mortality. I could kill you and it wouldn't bother me any more than shooting that dog. I don't like you. Some men just rub me that way, they're all dead though." His voice lowered to a whisper, "You ever look me in the eye like you did over there in the doorway, you are a dead man. If you have something against me you strap your gun on and meet me outside, but don't you ever stare at me like you are my equal."

He took a gulp of whiskey and cocked his head, "You got anything to say to me boy?" Ray lowered his eyes so as not to look into his and shook his head. "I can't hear you" Garth said in a deadly hiss.

"No" Ray said softly.

"No what? Garth insisted.

"No sir" Ray answered. Garth dropped his leg and let him pass.

That night as Ray lay in bed, he felt ashamed and

humiliated. He spent his last three years on the ranch learning to shoot. He was good at it, but good at shooting at rocks and cans and trees. He was smart enough to know the difference between that and shooting at a man who was shooting back. How fast was he? He didn't even know. He had never tested himself against anyone.

Garth had killed many men and seemed to enjoy it. Ray gritted his teeth as he went over and over in his mind the scene of Garth humiliating him and the fear he felt. It was like being trapped at close quarters by a rattlesnake, something you never forget. His mind went back to the ranch and his mother and his dad and all the things he learned from him. He missed them. He felt like a little boy who wanted to snuggle in his mother's arms and go to sleep. The hot tears flowed down his cheeks and he fell asleep.

2

The next morning was gray and damp with streaks of lightning in the distance. Jack Garth rose early with a slight hangover and went to the well to splash cold water on his face before breakfast. Several others were at the well with him talking about the day's activities. As Garth dried his face with a towel a sudden silence fell over the others and they quickly left. They did not want to be around when Garth saw him. Garth turned around to see Ray Williams step down from the porch wearing his gun. His eyes met Garth's with a determined intensity.

Garth's eyes went glassy as though he were in a trance. He stepped out into the open, "You're buzzard meat," he said through clenched teeth.

"That's a distinct possibility" Ray said softly. But Ray didn't care anymore. He felt a complete calm come over him. There was no more fear – a death was better than what he was going through now. He felt totally in control of the situation.

Garth wore a gleeful grin on his face relishing what was about to happen. He went for his familiar blink-of-the-eye draw, but a bullet tore through his chest before his hand ever touched his gun, a look of total surprise on his face as he dropped to his knees, then fell face down in the dirt.

A gust of wind blew, stirring up the dust as it began to drizzle rain. The men watching stood in awe at what they had just seen. A dead silence hung in the air. Ray looked almost bewildered as though he was surprised at his own speed. He was sure Gath would kill him. He was filled with mixed emotions; he knew Garth was a snake and deserved to die and was relieved to still be alive, but he also felt sadness at ending another human being's life.

Foreman Tom Hansen verified to the Sheriff that it was a fair fight. The sheriff warned Ray that now that he had killed Jack Garth in a gunfight, everyone who wanted a reputation would be gunning for him. Every young kid would dream about the fame he could achieve by killing him. Ray assured him that only a few people knew what happened, and he would not tell anyone about it. As far as he was concerned, killing a man was nothing to brag about. In fact it made him feel sick, like he wanted to throw up.

Ray's life had been turned upside down. He was not only on the run for killing those cowhands, but now he was on the run from his own reputation after killing Jack Garth. He now had to change locations. He would ride to Fort Worth and find a job. He had pay coming from the foreman and he had some money put away from his poker winnings.

He would stay another week or so until the foreman found a man to replace him. Over supper Logan Nash sat by Ray who informed him that he had to move on.

"I figured that" Logan said, sipping his coffee, "Where you headed?"

"I'm not sure" Ray said, "I was thinking of Fort Worth. It's kind of scary, I have never been on my own before."

"This is not good territory to be alone" Logan said.

The next day Logan said he was ready for a change and offered to accompany Ray to Fort Worth. Ray was thankful for the offer. It would be much easier for two to survive together, and Logan seemed so much more experienced than Ray and easy to get along with.

"I have a couple of friends who will be interested in joining us. I've rode with them before. We can teach you a lot about surviving on your own. It's always good to have friends you can count on. You never know when you're going to need their help later on," Logan said reassuringly. Logan informed foreman Hansen that he would be leaving when Ray did.

When foreman Hansen got his new men, Ray and Logan were ready to go. They would meet up with Logan's friends, Ike and Jake Holmen. It was about a day's ride to Fort Worth. When Ray met them he was very disappointed. He saw that they were both rather course men, both were impatient and not afraid of trouble but rather seemed to look for it. Ray was having second thoughts about his decision to ride with them. But it was too late to worry about that now. He would just have to make the most of the situation.

When they arrived in town, Ray and Logan got rooms in the hotel while Jake and Ike rode on. "Where are they going?" Ray asked.

"They know someone with a cabin outside of town," Logan answered. They found a place to eat.

Afterward Ray said, "Well let's get a room and get settled and go look for work." Logan stopped suddenly looking at Ray with a confused look on his face.

"You're not serious about looking for a job I hope?" Logan asked incredulously.

"Why wouldn't I be serious about getting a job. Isn't that why we came here?"

Logan looked at Ray as though he felt sorry for him. "I can't believe you're that damn innocent!" Ray stared at him wide eyed:

"What in the world are you talking about?" Ray said, confused.

Logan took a deep breath. "Look Ray, life is too

short to play society's silly games. We have to take what we want. I thought you understood that. It's an unwritten law: never trust anyone and you will never be disappointed. Don't you see, we're not where we are by choice. We were forced here."

Now Ray was beginning to see what he was driving at. "Look at you Ray," Logan went on. "You're here, on the run, because some cowhands killed your dad and burned down your home, which eventually ended up in killing your mother. And I was there when you killed Jack Garth. If anyone deserved to die, it was that overbearing monster!"

Ray felt a bitterness overwhelming him. "You're right I am an innocent sap!" He said. He began to see things in a different light. He saw Logan and the Holmen brothers as his true friends, his only friends. "I don't owe anybody anything," he said.

"Now listen to me. Jake and Ike are meeting with someone outside of town. The three of them have sized up this town and its bank. Jake mentioned it to me before and said they still needed someone good with a gun, someone fast, like you. I mentioned Jack Garth to them, but they didn't trust him. When I saw you outdraw him I knew you were the one we needed," Logan said, "That's why we're here."

Later that night, Jake and Ike Holmen came to Ray and Logan's room with the plan to take the bank in the morning when it first opened and be out of town before anyone knew what happened. The bank opened at 9 o'clock. Jake and Ike would arrive at the bank minutes before, while their friend, Carl Shultz, would ride to the bank moments later. Then Ray and Logan would casually walk over to the bank, all seemingly independent of each other.

There would be no nonsense. Ray and Logan would stand outside the bank in case they needed help inside, pretending to be having a serious discussion, Carl Shultz would stand inside the bank door while Jake and Ike carried out the holdup.

They would grab the money and be out of town before anyone realized that there was a hold-up. They would split up and each ride to Shultz's cabin. In the meantime Ray and Logan would casually walk back to their horses and ride out to Shultz's cabin where they would quickly split up the money. It was agreed that no one would be killed and there would be no gunfire that would draw attention during the hold up.

They all agreed on the plan. Then Jake and Ike rode back to Karl Shultz's cabin where they would wait until morning.

The next morning shortly before 9 o'clock, Jake and Ike Holmen arrived at the bank. Ray and Logan watched out their hotel window. Ray slept fitfully; he still could not shake the uneasy feeling he had about the other three men. A little later they watched Shultz ride up to the bank. "It's time," Logan said and they started walking to the bank. The three men entered the bank while Ray and Logan pretended to have a serious discussion just outside the door.

After several minutes, gunshots were heard, and the three men burst out the door and mounted their horses and rode off. Ray and Logan were walking back to their hotel for their horses as the sheriff and a deputy arrived. Moments later they were joined by two more deputies.

Ray and Logan waited awhile and then rode out to the cabin. There was no sign of anyone; they waited a while longer and realized that they had taken off with the money. Ray was furious with Logan. "How do I know you were not in on this"! Ray demanded.

Logan was clearly shaken. He tried to speak but couldn't find the words. "You set this up," Ray added.

Logan became angry. "If I were part of this, do you

think I'd be standing here arguing with you while they're gone with the money?" He snarled.

"Alright, alright" Ray said, throwing his hands up. "I'm sorry. We have to stick together and find them."

"And then kill them". Logan added

Ray and Logan cooled off and thought things out. It wasn't all that bad after all. "We're not implicated in the hold-up," Ray said thoughtfully.

Logan jerked his head around wide eyed. "And if we find them and kill them, the money's ours and   we're home free," he said.

"We don't even know how much money they got," Ray said.

"No we don't, but we know it was a lot," Logan added.

"They likely ran to the next town," Ray said.

"Let's find them" Logan said. "Let's go to the next town and look for them, and I think it's a foregone conclusion that when we find then, we kill them."

"Only if we have to," Ray said, remembering the sick feeling he had when he killed Garth.

After a week they finally talked to someone just outside the town of Green Meadows who described three men fitting the descriptions of Jake, Ike, and Shultz who were heading for Oklahoma with one other man they met, James Graff, a hired gunman. He last saw them in town at the saloon gambling at the card table, throwing money around. "They have rooms in the hotel across the street." The man left them with a final warning, "I don't know why you're looking for them, but I wouldn't tangle with these guys if I were you. They hired Graff, paying him lots of dough – for a reason."

Ray thanked him, and he and Logan went to town separately and each bought some food and shared a room in the hotel across the street from their hotel. They knew that they could not confront them without first knowing where the money was. They would watch for them while being very careful and confront them at the right time, keeping the element of surprise on their side. They would take turns watching from their hotel window while the other slept.

The next day Jake, Ike, and Shultz came to the hotel across the street. They knew they would have the money with them.

"Well this certainly makes things easier," Logan said.

Ray spoke. "But where's Graff? He's the main one we have to worry about. We can't make a move until we know where he is and eliminate him."

"That's going to have to fall on you," Logan said. "I may be a match for Ike and Jake and Shultz but certainly not for Graff. Are you sure you can take Graff?"

"How would I know?" Ray said.

"You're the fastest gun I ever saw," Logan said.

"But have you ever seen Graff draw?" Ray asked.

"No," Logan said.

"Neither have I," Ray said.

"That's what makes a gunfight so interesting" Ray said wryly. "You don't know who's going to win until one of you is dead."

Later that day, all plans were changed by Graff himself. He decided, instead of working for them, he would steal the money they stole.

He entered their hotel and knocked on the door to their room with their secret knock. They opened the door and Graff, seeing that Shultz was not there, asked where he was. They told him he was down the hall using the bathroom. Graff pulled his gun and told them to get the money quickly. Any trouble and he'd shoot both of them.

Ike reached under the bed and pulled out the saddlebag.

"Count it," Graff said.

Ike counted out $37,000. Meanwhile, Jake reached under the other side of the bed and pulled out a gun. Graff spun around and fired, hitting him in the throat. Ike threw his hands up, but Graff shot him in the chest. He grabbed the saddlebag and went out the door only to see Shultz hurrying down the hall. Graff shot him in the chest and not breaking stride he ran down the hall and out the door to his horse and rode away.

Ray and Logan watched him ride away.

"Well this is what we've been waiting for," Ray said.

They quickly got to their horses and pursued him to a cabin about a mile away. Ray and Logan watched him run into the cabin. They both got off their horses and walked toward the cabin. A shot rang out and Logan went down. He lay there and looked at Ray. Ray started toward him and Logan motioned for him to stay down.

"He got me in the shoulder," he said.

Ray went to the window of the cabin and yelled in. "Give us half and we'll leave," Ray said.

"Why would I do that when I can have it all?" Graff said from behind Ray.

Ray spun around and saw Graff standing there with a glassy look in his eyes that made Ray think of Jack Garth. "It's much less risky my way" Ray said."

"Risky for who?" Graff laughed.

"It's your choice," Ray said.

Both men faced each other. Graff grinned, "I think I'll take it all," he said, going for his gun.

Ray's bullet ripped into him before his hand ever touched his gun. Ray picked up the saddlebag with the money. Logan looked as if he didn't know what to expect next. His look said the money was all Ray's if Ray simply pulled the trigger one more time.

Ray walked over and stood over him: "I hope you're not looking for sympathy for that little scratch on your shoulder," Ray chuckled.

"No, I'm just relieved that you outdrew him. I wasn't all that sure you could," Logan said, getting up.

Ray looked over at Graff. "Neither was I." He helped Logan up and said, "We have to get you to a doctor."

When they arrived back in town they rode past the Sheriff's office. The sheriff was standing on the walkway with two deputies, watching them as they rode by. Ray nodded and the sheriff nodded back.

Ray and Logan stopped at the doc's office and had Logan's shoulder taken care of. It was not nearly as bad as Ray thought it was. The bullet didn't actually enter the shoulder but only deeply grazed it. They found out that the bank teller was killed during the hold up. They figured they had better ride if Logan was able, before things started to catch up with them. They went back to their hotel and got some of their things and rode on to Dallas.

The town of Cool Waters was wide open. There was law there but very lax. Laws were broken right in front of the sheriff and his deputies with almost no consequences. The sheriff was a good man dedicated to his job but was overwhelmed by the job and his lack of help, and his two deputies were somewhat intimidated by the thugs in the town.

When Ray and Logan rode into town, they were met by sheriff James Rollin who said he would take their guns. Ray looked around at the men who still had their guns. "Shouldn't you take everybody's guns?" he asked.

Logan held his hands up. "Look, we're not looking for trouble."

"Then you won't mind me taking your guns," the sheriff said.

"That kind of puts us at a disadvantage doesn't it?" Ray said.

Sheriff Rollin looked both men over. "You have a point there," he said, "My deputies don't always do their job, but deputies are hard to come by in this town, so I have to settle for what I can get. I'll let you keep your guns until I confiscate the rest of the guns. But then you will have to give them up," he said, letting them know that he meant business.

"Fair enough," Ray said. "Where can we get some hot food? We may just be passing through."

"Over at the saloon. There's a back area that serves food. It's nothing to brag about, but it's hot," Sheriff Rollins said with a big grin.

The food wasn't all that bad. The town's minister, Reverend Samuel Jansen, was being served by the waitress. Ray couldn't help being drawn to her. She had a rather plain beauty, and he noticed that she had dirt under her fingernails. He couldn't take his eyes off of her.

Somebody nudged him. "You must be new in town. I haven't seen you around before. That girl you're staring at, I wouldn't gawk too long, that's the sheriff's daughter."

The minister gave her some pieces of literature entitled "The Meaning of Life" that she was to give out. She took it and put it in her bag and refilled his coffee cup.

Someone from across the room said something with a snicker and someone whispered in Logan's ear that she was Sheriff Rollin's daughter. The man nodded and walked off.

Logan's words brought Ray out of his trance. "It's pretty obvious that you are taken with that girl."

"Is it that obvious?" Ray asked.

"You heard what that guy said. She's the sheriff's daughter."

Ray and Logan got two rooms at the hotel. They met in Ray's room and split up the $37,000. Ray counted out $18,500 and threw Logan's share on the dresser.

Logan asked Ray if he would give him some pointers on using a gun. Ray said he would be glad to, and, for the next five days, he spent two hours a day showing Logan how to shoot and draw a gun. After that Logan practiced on his own. He became very good at both drawing his gun and hitting a target.

3

After a few days, Ray and Logan found a job at a ranch not far from town. They didn't need the money but needed something to do. Ray was trying to work up nerve to ask the Sheriff's daughter out for a picnic. He found out her name was Amber Marie. She worked at the diner and she helped the minister on Sundays.

Finally, he decided it was time, come do or die, to ask her to ride out for a picnic. He was a mess that day. He felt very awkward and nervous. To his great relief, she accepted but said he had to ask her father. Now he was really nervous!

Later that day, he worked up enough nerve to go to the sheriff's office. The sheriff was sitting at his desk. "What brings you here?" he asked.

Ray looked down at his shoes. "Well sir, he began.

Sheriff Rollins cut in, "Ah excuse me Ray, but are you talking to me or to the floor?"

"To you sir, ah I wanted to ask you if it would be all right, sir, for me to take your daughter, Amber, on a picnic this Sunday, sir."

"Well, that would be fine with me. But of course you do know that you will have to escort her to church first," he said.

"O yes, of course sir." Ray said.

"Before I answer I must ask, are you sure you're up to it?"

Ray frowned, "Pardon me sir?"

"It looks to me like you're on the verge of a nervous breakdown." Sheriff Rollins burst out in laughter.

"What?" Ray looked confused.

"If you would have called me sir one more time I think I would have been sick!"

Ray was confused. "What are you talking about?"

"Relax, I was just having some fun with you," Sheriff Rollin said. "Amber was over earlier today and told me you were coming and why you were coming."

Ray couldn't help smiling. "Are you kidding?" he said. "I was on the verge of a heart attack."

"Well that's my little girl and you better be good to her; you better not hurt her."

Ray's smile broadened, "No sir, I'll treat her with utmost respect."

The date went very well. Ray attended the church service with the sheriff and Amber Marie. Ray was moved by the church service. The pastor talked as though Christ was real and involved in our lives.

Ray accepted Jesus Christ as his Lord and Savior that morning. Ray had always been religious, but he had never made that step. Now it seemed to make it all so real. Now he felt the presence of God. The minister gave him the passages in John 6:37: "All those the Father gives me will come to me, and whoever comes to me I will never drive away," and Revelation 3:20: "Here I am! I stand at the door and knock. If anyone hears my voice and opens the door, I will come in and eat with that person, and they with me." Ray felt that God did come into his life. He took Jesus at His word and trusted Him and vowed He would be faithful. He knew his life would be different.

The picnic also went very well. In fact, Ray fell in love. They found a place in the shade with a beautiful view and he spread out the blanket. She had brought ham sandwiches and homemade blueberry pie. She brought extra treats for the rabbits, birds, and squirrels that came around and even some sugar lumps for the horses.

They laughed and enjoyed feeding the animals while they ate the ham sandwiches. "You seem to be really enjoying yourself. I was worried you would be bored," she said.

"Actually, I'm having a very good time and your cooking is very good," he said, putting the last of his sandwich into his mouth.

"I was very happy to see you go forward in the church service," she said, while cutting the pie and putting a piece on his plate.

"I have believed in Jesus for some time, but I'd never given myself completely to Him and made a public confession until today," Ray said.

"It's the greatest decision anyone could ever make," Amber said.

They read from the Bible, the Gospel of John, and discussed what they were reading for two hours: God taking upon Himself humanity so he could communicate with us and also die for our sins as mankind's representative and rise from the dead also as our representative, showing that God the Father accepted Jesus' death as payment for our sins.

"Many are offended by the violent and horrible death of Christ, but sin is a terrible business and it had to be dealt with in a horrible way. Christ had to take the punishment we deserve and vindicate God's holiness. God is holy and God is love. His holiness had to be satisfied and upheld by the judgment of sin. God spared the sinners He loved us by taking the judgment upon Himself in the person of His Son Jesus Christ" Ray said. It was obvious the Holy Spirit was leading Ray in what to say. He couldn't have come up with all that by himself.

"This is the message of the Gospel, meaning Good News, that our sins have all been paid for and all we have to do is accept this and place our faith in Christ," she responded.

Then they prayed that their lives would count for Christ. Ray said he felt that God had work for him to do but wasn't sure what it was. She said God would reveal His will to him. She was sure that God had given her work to do with Pastor Jansen.

Then they had the blueberry pie she made. "Well, since you are having such a good time, I hope you will ask me to another picnic, many more, as a matter of fact" she said.

"I will definitely do that," he said. She looked into his eyes and reached over and touched his hand. He looked very uncomfortable. "We better go," he said abruptly. She was very surprised at his reaction. They picked up the picnic stuff and headed home.

In the wagon going back to town, she asked, "Why are you so uptight? Why do I make you so nervous?"

Ray shrugged his shoulders and said casually, "Because I'm not worthy to be near you, and I'm afraid you're going to realize that."

"I'll be the judge of that," Amber said.

Sheriff Rollins grew up around the law his whole life. His father and grandfather had been lawman. His grandfather had been killed in a shootout with bank robbers. He admired his father and wanted to be like him. He was a lawman through and through. He would say, "This world would be hell without the law." He believed the greatest law was the new birth because it ruled from within a person's heart.

The founding fathers knew this and many times they called the nation to repentance and prayer. They believed that men had to be ruled either by the Bible or by tyrants and that the greatest asset to a free people was the Bible. George Washington, our first president, insisted upon being sworn in with his hand on the Bible, which has been followed by all presidents after him, and when he had done this he bent down and kissed the Bible.

Rollins' wife died while giving birth to Amber Marie. Her last request to Rollins was that he would bring Amber up for the Lord. Rollins gave her a loving Christian home and led her to receive Christ at a very early age.

When they drove up to the Sheriff's office, the sheriff was arguing with four men who had their guns on and did not want to turn them in. Ray helped Amber off the wagon and into the sheriff's office. Then Ray walked out and stood next to the sheriff.

Ray looked at the four men. "It's time to turn your guns in boys."

They laughed, "Are you two going to take all four of us on?" one of them said.

Ray replied to them. "We're hoping we won't have to, but that's up to you. We're just doing our job gentlemen, and we hope you'll cooperate with us, but if not, then make your move."

Then Ray heard a voice call out, "There's three of us. Ray smiled as he recognized the voice. It was Logan's.

"Well, gentlemen, it's time to turn in your guns," Ray said smiling. The men began to have second thoughts as one of them recognized Ray. He put his hands up and the others followed. "I didn't recognize you at first, Mr. Williams," he said,

"This is Ray Williams," he said to those with him. They offered their guns to Sheriff Rollins. Then, looking at Ray, the man said, "We may be stupid but ain't crazy!"

"Just what I don't need, recognition," Ray muttered to himself. He figured that his days in this town were numbered. He looked over at Logan. "Time to move on."

"Move on where?" asked the sheriff.

"Anywhere but here," Ray said. "Away from my

reputation."

"No," said Sheriff Rollins. "This is exactly where you both belong – as my deputies, where you will be protected by the law. Don't you see, your reputation when used for good ended what could have been a gunfight. I'll see to it that you both get extra pay." He put his hand on Ray's shoulder. "This is where you're needed, where you will be appreciated."

Ray smiled and said, "Does this mean I can go on more picnics with your daughter?"

"Well, from what she told me, I think that is a definite yes," Rollin said.

The next day they put up more posters warning that all guns must be turned in by the end of that day or folks would be arrested. It wasn't surprising that no one turned in their guns.

Ray went into the sheriff's office. There were three wealthy businessmen there telling Rollins that law and order had to be restored or this town was going to dry up and die from too much violence.

Ray nodded to them and stood in front of the sheriff's desk. He put both hands on his desk and leaned forward and chose his words very carefully. "Just how determined are you to get law and order in this town. We're responsible for the safety of these people."

The sheriff looked around at the three businessmen, "Very determined," he said looking Ray in the eye.

Ray held his eyes with his. "Then we're going to have to be tougher on enforcing the law."

The sheriff closed his eyes. "Look," Ray said, "I don't want violence any more than you do, but I don't see how we can avoid it. The people have to know we mean business or they're going to run all over us. Sometimes it takes violence to prevent violence. To protect the good guys you have to stop the bad guys. He looked over at the businessmen, "That's just the way it is gentlemen."

They nodded their heads understandingly. One of them said, "Would you please excuse us a moment?"

The three of them walked out the door and had a short conference on the walkway. Logan came in from the other room. Rollin's two deputies, Brad and Craig, followed him. The sheriff said, "You two won't have to deal with the violence. But there are things that need to be done so the rest of us are free to deal with the law-breakers. You take care of the office and jail cells, clean, cook, and watch the prisoners.

The businessmen came back inside. Their spokesman said: "All right gentlemen. You have our full support. We know the danger level will go up considerately, so we'll raise your pay and give whatever other support you might need. You have free reign to do whatever you need to do, and we'll protect you from any legal ramifications.

The next morning, bright and early, five men rode in wearing their guns without stopping at the sheriff's office to turn them in. Logan turned from watching out the window, looking like he had a bitter taste in his mouth. He held up five fingers. "Five men wearing guns just rode by," he said.

"Well, I guess we'll be testing our new policy," Rollin said.

Ray, Rollins, and Logan walked down the street. They could see that four men went into the saloon and one man went down to the blacksmith's. The sheriff looked at Logan, "You take the man at the blacksmith's, and we'll take the men in the bar."

Logan nodded and went on down to the blacksmith's stable. Ray and Sheriff Rollins stood outside the door of the saloon. "Ready? The sheriff asked. Ray nodded. Both men walked in the door. The four men stood at the bar with their drinks. Ray and Logan stood behind them.

"You gentlemen forgot to drop your guns off at my office," the sheriff said in a loud voice.

"It sure looks that way" one man laughed. Everybody in the bar laughed. Ray slapped him on the side of his head with his left hand, knocking his hat off and almost knocking him down. "You heard the sheriff. Now take your guns off while you're still able to," Ray said calmly. The man hesitated, "Now," Ray said, "while you still can."

The man was furious. The bartender in front of him said something that changed his expression from anger to fear. The man looked over his shoulder. "I'm sorry, I didn't know who you were, Mr. Williams." Ray was surprised that his reputation followed him this far.

"I'm not going to tell you again," Ray said very calmly.

The man looked at the men next to him, and all four men dropped their gun belts. Ray looked at the sheriff. The sheriff looked at Ray and shook his head and smiled. "Well, I'll tell you what I'm going to do," Rollins said. "Because you were cooperative, I'm not going to run you in." Then looking around he added: "And the rest of you men, I'm going to extend the deadline to turn in your guns until the end of today. And take this to heart: after today, anyone wearing guns in the city limits will be arrested and jailed."

Logan entered the door behind them carrying the fifth man's gun belt with a look of triumph mixed with relief. Ray put his arm around the man whose hat he had knocked off. Ray did not like humiliating anyone. He spoke so every one could hear him. "Thank you for turning in your guns. I apologize for knocking your hat off, but the next time pay attention when the sheriff speaks. And the rest of you understand this: from now on you had all better respect the law, you have all been warned."

As the three men walked back to the sheriff's office, Logan said, "So far this has been a pretty good day."

"How did it go with you?" Ray asked.

"Good, he said. "I told him that he'd forgotten to turn over his gun. He was fine with it but was worried that if we were confiscating all guns he might not get his right gun back. So I told him to put a little scratch on the handle. He did and then gave me his gun." He laughed and asked how it went with them.

"Ray took charge," Rollins said. "He was very intimidating. Hell, he even scared me, and I was on his side." He chuckled. Then looking at Ray he said, "Here we see again how your reputation prevented a lot of violence."

But Ray was bothered by the fact that the bartender knew who he was. He did not want to move on to another town. He liked his job here, but most of all he liked Amber Marie. He feared something spoiling it.

The sheriff seemed to notice that something was bothering Ray. "It's going to work out fine. We sent a strong message today. I think the hardest part is over."

"I hope you're right," Ray said, giving a rather strained smile.

After a few days, their jobs became routine. The sheriff stayed in his office most of the day as guns were turned over by people entering town and picked up as they were leaving again. Ray and Logan made their rounds checking for lawbreakers three times a day. The other two deputies, Chris and Tom, took care of the jail, cleaning and cooking and made rounds checking on shut-ins who were sick and others who needed help.

One Sunday after Church services, Ray took Amber Marie on a picnic up near Indian Springs. They talked about marriage while eating. Afterward, they both sat in the shade of a tree reading from the Bible for about an hour. Afterward, he fell asleep and she tickled his nose with long blades of grass. Suddenly He sat up as Logan rode up.

"You are needed back in town, there's trouble." Ray helped Amber onto the wagon and followed Logan.

Back in town, Ray helped Amber off the wagon and the two of them entered the sheriff's office.

There was a man in jail gritting his teeth. "You have no idea what you're in for. My dad will send his men here and you'll wish you were never born."

Logan walked over to his cell, "If you don't shut your mouth, you will wish you were never born."

Ray gave sheriff Rollins a questioning look. "Well," Rollins began, "two men stood outside the door and yelled that they were ready to turn in their guns. When Craig opened the door, one of the men shot him and I shot the gunman. His friend," he said pointing at the jail cell, "surrendered and yelled to someone behind him to go and get his father."

"And Craig?" Ray asked.

The sheriff shook his head. "We don't know yet. The doctor's watching him. He said he should know in the morning."

Ray looked grim. "Do I dare ask who his father is

"Prescott Monahan, a very wealthy and powerful rancher with a 2,000 acre ranch in Fort Worth, about ten miles away, who is very devoted to his son." The sheriff pointed at his cell. "Oh, and by the way, the father's thinking of running for governor."

"Great." Ray said.

"Yes and my father will send a dozen men here to get me," the prisoner, Derek Monahan, said.

"That won't do you any good because they'll find you dead," Brad said.

"Just let me go and my dad will forget the whole thing. Otherwise, he will tear this town apart."

The sheriff replied back. "We might have taken you up on that, son, if you hadn't shot my deputy."

4

They had to come up with a plan being there were only four of them. They'd have to split up. They didn't want to be grouped together and be easy targets. The sheriff would sit outside the door of the sheriff's office. Brad would stay inside the jailhouse. Brad came up with the idea to point rifles out three of the windows of the Sheriff's office as though there were men holding them.

It was a very hot night. Ray and Logan made the rounds checking out the town. The minutes crept by until the morning light began to break when three men rode into town.

They stopped suddenly by the sheriff's office and looked all around the town, checking it out, then turned around and left as fast as they came in.

Ray and Logan made their way to the sheriff, who was standing as though expecting trouble any time. They knew they were coming back with an army of men. They had to think fast.

Logan and Brad were each to take a rifle with several extra rounds down the street behind a couple barrels where they could fire at long range. They were to wait for Rollins' signal. Ray and Sheriff Rollins would stay where they were and shoot at close range and take as many as possible, while Logan and Brad picked them off at long range.

As they waited, the minutes seemed like hours. Finally the gang showed up in the early morning. Eleven men rode in with Prescott Monahan. No one said anything, but it was very clear that there would be bloodshed. Ray and Sheriff Rollins stood side by side. The men in front of them seemed nervous.

"Gentlemen," the sheriff said.

"You know why we're here," Prescott Monahan said.

Sheriff Rollins gave the signal: two rifle shots from Logan and Brad rang out and two men went down. Ray and the sheriff drew their guns and began shooting. They were greatly aided by Prescott's men shooting at the rifles pointing out the windows. The gang had wasted their bullets on empty windows while Ray and the Sheriff shot down six of them! Prescott escaped but eight of his men did not. Prescott and two other men rode off.

Ray had the eerie feeling that they were being protected. The question now was would they be back? As long as they held his son they could count on them being back, and they had to be ready. It was only a matter of time. Later that day they got more good news: deputy Craig was going to be okay.

About a week later, when things were pretty peaceful, the doctor asked Ray to bring some medicine out to the Fergusson house. Earlier, the doctor had ridden out to see Mrs. Fergusson, an elderly woman whose husband was away, and found that she had a high fever. He rode back in his buggy to get her some medicine, but when he stepped down to get out he twisted his ankle. The doctor's assistant was gone for the day, so the doctor sent his seven-year-old son to the sheriff's office to tell him that he needed someone to bring Mrs. Fergusson's medicine to her.

Ray had just gotten back from breaking up a fight at the saloon. Bob, who would have normally done this, was visiting Craig, who was recovering from his wound.

So Ray volunteered to bring the medicine to her. He was informed that he needed to bring her some food as well.

Amber dropped off some chicken soup she had made, as Ray was ready to go. He put it in his saddlebag and rode to the General Store to pick up some groceries. When he came out of the store, a storm was stirring in the distance. He put the groceries in three large saddlebags, then untied his horse as a cool breeze blew up patches of dust. A short distance away, he saw a dusty cowboy, holding a poster in his hand, get off his horse. Ray could see him tense as he glanced from the poster to Ray and started walking toward him. Ray dropped the rein and stepped out from behind his horse. He could feel the blood surging in his temples.

The man walked over and stood there holding the poster.

"Bounty hunter?" Ray asked quietly.

He threw the poster at Ray's feet and nodded. The determined look in the man's eyes told Ray that soon one of them would be dead. Ray noticed under all the dust that it was just a boy standing there, maybe nineteen or twenty. Ray remembered that he was nineteen when he killed Jack Garth.

"How old are you?" Ray asked, sounding more like a father than a deadly foe.

"What difference does that make?" The bounty hunter snapped back, rather nervously.

"It makes a lot of difference to me son," Ray said. "In a few minutes I have to kill you, and I would like to think that you lived long enough to fulfill some of your dreams and are ready to meet your Maker"

The bounty hunter swallowed hard. For a fleeting moment Ray could see a look of bewilderment in his eyes that said maybe he had bitten off more than he could chew.

A deadly calm came over Ray. "You're scared son,"

he said. "Your hand is shaking, but that's all right. I'm scared too. So why don't we just back off and go our separate ways."

A look of relief came into the boy's eyes but was quickly replaced by the one of iron determination. "I can't do that," he said. "I have a wife and kid to feed, and work is scarce."

Ray knew that there was a $5000 reward offered on that poster for him dead or alive. Ray held up his right hand so the bounty hunter could see it and slowly reached into his saddlebag with his left hand and took out two one-hundred-dollar coins and dropped them on the ground. "Here, take this." Ray said. "I know it's not $5000 but at least you'll get to spend it."

He looked at the money then back at Ray. "Take it son," Ray said. The boy's fingers twitched. The tension was getting to Ray. He hissed at the boy, "You're not ready for me boy. Pick up the money.

The boy let out a deep breath releasing all his tension. His shoulders sagged. He seemed exhausted. He stared down at the money. "You think I'm a coward."

"Pick up the money and get out of here," Ray said. The tension mounted.

The boy picked up the money and put it in his pocket. He stood there as though he wanted to say something. "Get out of here," Ray said. Ray mounted his horse and rode to the outskirts of town and looked back. The boy was gone. A light rain began to fall as he rode on. A cold wind chilled him to the bone. The hot tears flowed down his face.

It was dark when Ray arrived at the Fergusson home and delivered the medicine, the groceries, and the soup Amber had sent, along with some literature from the reverend. Mrs. Fergusson wearily opened the door for him. She had been in bed. She was weak and tired. He told her to go back to bed and he would bring her some very good soup that Amber had sent. He put the groceries away while she took her medicine. She said her husband would be back tomorrow morning.

Ray handed her the literature from the pastor while he dished her up some soup. He waited while she ate her soup. Ray asked her if she would like him to read from the Bible. She said she would like that. She closed her eyes as he read.

After about an hour, he thought she was sleeping. But when he stopped reading, she opened her eyes and asked if he would read some more. He read for another hour, until daylight. She was asleep. He knew her husband would be back soon, so he read the Bible by himself until her husband came home.

Her husband was startled at first when Ray opened the door for him. Ray explained what happened and said he thought it best not to leave her alone again. He was very thankful and agreed to stay with her while she was sick.

The next day Ray met with the sheriff and told him what happened with the bounty hunter, and they both wondered if Prescott Monahan had sent him. They both realized that Monahan could cause a lot trouble for them. Ray told the sheriff that he wondered if it was time to move on.

"Where to?" Sheriff Rollins asked.

"I don't know" Ray said.

"Then its best to stay where you're at, among friends. You're not going to abandon me now when we're in the middle of a war with Monahan's men are you?"

"No, of course not. I just feel trapped," Ray said.

"You're not trapped. Stay here and we'll work this out," Rollins said. "We have a chance to turn this town around, but I'm going to need your help."

The next day the stage was several hours late, and Ray was sent out to check on it. He found the stagecoach near the border of Oklahoma; a wheel had rolled off the axle. Five Indian warriors nearby were watching. When Ray neared them, he gave the signal for friendship that he learned from the tribe near where he grew up. One warrior rode out to meet him. Ray held up the palm of his right hand, showing him the scar where the cut was made to make him a blood brother with the tribe years before.

They followed Ray to the stagecoach, where the driver and passengers were fighting panic. Ray held up his hands. "It's all right; they're friends."

One of the drivers instinctively placed his hand on his gun. "I would definitely not do that," Ray said, holding his hands up to the Indians, signaling that it was under control. Then, turning to the driver, he said very deliberately, "These are Arapaho dog soldiers; they're here to help. Don't provoke them. Any one of them could tear your heart out with his bare hands."

Ray motioned to the Indians that he needed help lifting the coach so the wheel could be put back on. The leader among them motioned to them and the four others jumped off their horses and easily lifted the coach while a driver slid the wheel on and put the peg back in.

The drivers got on and one of them took the reins. The Indians mounted their horses and Ray held up his right hand to show them the scar of brotherhood. Each Indian nodded as they rode by him.

Back in town Ray explained what happened and urged the people not to consider these Indians savages. "They have a different culture; we're savages to them. Our first instinct should not be to shoot but to communicate with them. I'm not saying they're all friendly. They should be approached cautiously, but don't be so quick to think the worst."

The next day the sheriff sent his deputy to tell Ray he wanted to see him "on important business."

"That sounds serious," Ray said to the deputy.

"I don't know; he wouldn't tell me anything," the deputy said. "I was told it was best that no one knew what was happening."

Ray laughed a nervous laugh. "Now, that really sounds serious, I better get going."

In the sheriff's office, sheriff Rollins and Logan and his two deputies were waiting. Ray walked in, looking around. "What's going on?"

"Well, you know our little problem here," the sheriff said, pointing toward the prisoner. Ray nodded. "Well," Rollins went on, "I was thinking that instead of waiting for the circuit judge to come here, what if one of us brought him to the circuit judge in Little Rock? We might avoid a confrontation with Monahan's gang and a lot of bloodshed." Ray looked around at all the faces and nodded. "When do I leave?"

"Tonight," Rollins said. "You do see why we have to send you, right? If he got away, this town would be a laughingstock. This is an important mission. In a couple days we'll let the word out what's going on, So Monahan will know there's no use coming here to break him out. We'll send a man with you if you want."

"No," Ray said. "The fewer men involved, the better."

"We'll tell Amber you went to see your brother in Abilene," Rollins said.

Ray prepared for the day's ride. He asked Logan to watch over Amber Marie. He remembered Logan had once told him, "Never trust anyone, and you'll never be disappointed." But he felt he could trust Logan with his life, and he could trust him with protecting Amber.

When it was dark, Ray brought Derek outside. "I'm going to give it to you straight." You give me any trouble, and you might not make it to Little Rock."

He put Derek on a horse and handcuffed his left

hand to the saddle horn between his legs, allowing his right hand to hold the reigns.

Derek muttered under his breath. "You better hope my dad doesn't have men watching this town for a move like this. If my dad and his men catch you, I'm going to enjoy what they'll to do to you."

"I've already thought of that, and I can assure you that you'll not enjoy what they do to me because you'll be dead." That shut Derek up.

The trip was slow, tedious, and uneventful until they got within a couple of miles of Little Rock. Ray spotted a couple of Monahan's men during the day and figured they'd have to try something that night.

When it was near nightfall, they stopped and made camp for the night. Ray made a fire. Then in the light of the fire, he made what appeared to be two beds with nobody in them. Ray pointed his gun at his prisoner and motioned for him to get on his horse. Then they got back on the trail and rode to Little Rock under the stars, hoping their little diversion would slow his pursuers down while they rode to the town.

On the way Ray, witnessed to Derek about God's love and Christ's sacrificial death on the cross and His resurrection. At first Darek was offended, but after some thought he thanked Ray for his concern. After that, he was very quiet and in deep thought for the rest of the trip.

That night, Ray dropped his prisoner off and spent the night in the back room of the sheriff's office while the sheriff and two deputies guarded the prisoner till morning. A U. S. Marshal would be there the next day and Ray would have to give witness.

When the Marshall arrived in town, Ray was awakened by a deputy who brought him a cup of coffee. The next day, Ray gave his testimony and the Marshal took Derek into custody. It was near dark and Ray prepared to head back to Dallas. The U. S. Marshall and the sheriff of

Little Rock thanked Ray as he mounted his horse.

He rode rapidly through the cool, clear night in deep thought about Darek. When he had travelled to about half a mile from his destination in Dallas, three riders approached him and opened fire. One of them hit Ray in the side, and he fell from his horse. He could see in the distance under a full moon and bright starry sky two shadowy figures. Thinking he may be dead, they slowly approached him.

When they were close enough, he fired on both of them. One of them went down. A bullet grazed Ray's head as he hit the second man. He was losing a lot of blood from the wound in his side. When Ray stood up he was woozy and staggered to his horse. He felt very thankful that the wound wasn't deeper, and he was also aware that if the bullet that grazed his head had been a fraction closer, he wouldn't be worrying about the wound in his side because he'd be dead.

He took so much effort to mount his horse that he was left weak and feeling faint. He rode on slowly, losing consciousness until everything went black and he fell off his horse. When he came to, He was looking into the face of the Arapaho Indian who had helped him with the stagecoach. He was relieved that he gave the sign of the cross that Ray had taught him and he had taught his warriors.

They put Ray on his horse and led him to their village where they made a bandage of herbs and placed it on his wound and nursed him back to health after three days during which he slept most of the time. When he had gained enough strength to ride again, he thanked them with the sign language they had worked out between them. Ray was especially thankful to God for watching over him. After eating a little, he headed back to Dallas.

It was near noon when Ray rode into town. Sheriff Rollins was sitting on the walkway in front of his office greeting men as they turned in their guns. When the sheriff saw Ray, he yelled for Logan to come out the door. Logan helped Ray off his horse and tied it to the hitching post. Amber came out the door as he stepped onto the walkway.

Rollins wanted to know about the trial and what took Ray so long. Ray explained the results of the trial and the conflict with Monahan's men and how he had been shot and the Arapaho tribe had brought him to their village and helped him to recover. Amber inspected his wound. They were all glad that he was back and the problem with Prescott Monahan was finally over.

Rollins was happy to see him. They were all worried when he didn't return when they expected. He could not resist giving him a hard time and said he would give Ray a couple days to recover fully. "But don't think you're not going to earn your pay after that. I'm not going to put up with any goldbricking. We have a town to bring law and order to," he kidded.

Amber took a look at his wounded side and moaned. "The first thing we have to do is get you to see the doctor, and I mean right now."

Ray patted her on the shoulder. "Take it easy," he said, "It may look like a pretty crude job of doctoring me up, but believe me they know their herbs and natural medicines. I can assure you that it is a lot better than it looks."

Logan and Amber helped him to the doctor's office. The doctor said the wound looked good and that what he needed now was lots of rest.

After a couple days, Ray was able to get around fairly well. He was able to sit in front of the sheriff's office while men turned in their guns, and he would take the wagon down for supplies while others loaded and unloaded it. In the meantime, Prescott Monahan stayed away from town but still held a grudge. He told his men that he would bide his time; they couldn't help his son now. He felt he owed Ray for bringing Derek to trial where he was sentenced to hang.

After another week Ray was back to normal and making his rounds in town. But change was clearly in the air. His concern was for Amber. He knew he could never settle down with her and have their own home and have children just outside of town as they had planned. He wondered how it would end for him, but he knew he didn't want her to be in any danger when it happened.

Ray also knew that it was only a matter of time until Sheriff Rollins would be ordered to arrest him. He wanted to avoid that confrontation. He knew he couldn't draw against him and didn't want to be hanged. So moving on was the only way open for him.

5

That Sunday in church Ray was thrilled to see Logan give his life to Christ. Logan and Ray had been going through the Scriptures on the new birth. Logan said he wanted to be sure that it was real. Ray assured him that it was. He said he knew it was real not only because of his own experience but because he saw it in the lives of many others. The minister gave Logan a Bible, and he had regular Bible studies with Ray.

A few days later it happened. Sheriff Rollins called him into his office. Ray sensed something was brewing. When he walked into the sheriff's office, Rollin's was sitting at his desk looking haggard and tired. He threw the papers ordering him to arrest Ray on the table. Their eyes met for several moments.

"Now what?" Ray asked. "I can't draw on you, and I know what a stickler you are on doing your job. I certainly don't want to hang."

Rollins stiffened up suddenly. "What? Are you crazy? I'm not going to arrest you. For what, defending yourself?" Ray walked over to the window and looked out.

"Just ride away," Rollins said. I'll deal with the consequences."

"And Amber?" Ray asked.

"Oh God!" Rollins said closing his eyes. "I'll explain it to her. I want you to know under any other circumstances I would have been thrilled with having you marry her. Maybe later, if things work out, you can send for her, I'll make sure she gets there."

Ray told Rollins he would wait until he found a replacement for him.

"You mean replacements for the two of you don't you? You know Logan is going to insist on going with you."

Logan proved sheriff Rollins right that same day. Ray explained to him the situation and said he'd have to move on to another town where he wasn't known.

"When do we leave?" Logan asked.

"Look." Ray said. I would love to have your company, but for your sake I think you should stay here. Being on the run is no life for anyone; I certainly would not have chosen it. Stay here. The town is pretty well cleaned up, and you have a good job here with Rollins. Put down roots, get married, have a family. It's going to be a good town; grow with it. Run for mayor or governor. Who knows what's in your future?"

Logan held up his hands. "Someone has to stop you before you make me president. I have one question for you. When do we leave?" Then with a big smile he added, "You do know the only reason you have made it this far is because I was with you? You wouldn't last one day on your own."

Ray shook his head. "Its getting pretty thick in here, isn't it, mommy?"

Logan put his hand on Ray's shoulder. "I don't think you can stay out of trouble without me," he kidded.

"All right, you can come along," Ray said. "Either that or I'm going to have to pull the wagon up and get a shovel to clean up the manure you're spreading around." Both of them laughed heartily at that.

About two weeks later two friends of Ray rode into town. Ray hadn't seen them since his school days. They were brothers and former Texas Rangers. When they met Ray on the street, they all did double takes, surprised to see each other.

"I thought you two joined the Texas Rangers," Ray said. "I thought I'd never see you again."

The two were Don and Roger Travis. "Well nothing lasts forever," Don said.

"After four years it's time to move on," Roger added.

"So what brings you here," Ray asked.

It was Roger who answered him. "Time to settle down in one area. Too much travelling in the Rangers." "What have you been up to?"

Ray explained how his parents were killed and he was on the run for killing their killers and then for killing Jack Garth.

"So, you guys will be looking for jobs," Logan said, nudging Ray, And you're former Texas Rangers."

"And you're looking to settle down in one area," Ray added.

"Sounds like you guys have already found us a job," Roger said.

Ray smiled. "Yes, and a very good job. We are both deputies for Sheriff James Rollins, and we have to move on for the reasons I explained to you. The town has a law that guns must be turned in before entering town, making it a lot easier to keep the law. The pay is good and the sheriff is a good man."

"We thought we'd try Oklahoma City," Logan said.

"When are you leaving?" asked Don.

Now it was Logan's turn to smile. "As soon as we find replacements for us."

"Let's go see the sheriff and I'll introduce you," Ray said, pointing to the sheriff's office.

Ray and Logan brought them to the sheriff's office and introduced them to him and his deputies. Sheriff Rollins asked a lot of questions and showed them around town with Ray and Logan. "You have Ray and Logan's recommend- ation, and that's good enough for me." He shook their hands and said, "You have the job."

That night in the sheriff's office, Ray and Rollins and Logan knelt in prayer and thanksgiving for God's leading.

The next day, Ray and Logan stopped to say good-bye to the minister. Reverend Samuel Jansen told them that he'd be praying for them and encouraged them to read a chapter of Scripture in the morning and at night. Ray informed him that he and Logan already did that, but now they will do two chapters in the morning and two chapters at night. Next they stopped at the Arapaho tribe to let them know that they were moving on to Oklahoma.

They arrived in Oklahoma late the next day in the town of Pleasant Meadows. After finding a hotel room, they looked the town over. They stopped in at the sheriff's office and introduced themselves and told him that they were new in town and wondered about work. The sheriff's name was Martin Ford and he asked what they did in Dallas. When he was told that they were deputies for Sheriff James Rollins in Cool Waters, he seemed interested in them.

"It shouldn't be hard to find work, maybe at the bank or guards for the stage coach. Let me think about it a couple days and ask around. You can sleep here at the jailhouse if you need a place to sleep," he said.

"We have rooms at the hotel," said Logan, "but thanks for the offer."

"Like I said, give me a couple days and I'll get back to you," sheriff Ford said.

Ray nodded his head. "Good enough."

Sheriff Ford's father was a minister. Ford was converted at twenty-one and wanted to train to be a minister. But God had a different plan. One day he was passing through Pleasant Meadows where he got a room in the hotel, but he couldn't sleep because of all the gunfire down the street.

He Got up and walked over to the sheriff's office and said his name was Martin Ford and wanted to complain to the sheriff about the wild gunfire. He was informed that the gunfire was coming from the saloon and that the man he was talking to, whose name was Gus, wasn't really the Sheriff. He was only kind of filling in until they hired a Sheriff.

The problem was that no one wanted the job. "So, you just let them run wild like this?" Ford asked.

"What can I do? I'm not a trained lawman," Gus replied.

"Neither am I,: Ford said, "but…" He left abruptly and went back to his hotel room, strapped on his gun, and walked down to the saloon.

He went in and found two drunken men forcing a young terrified woman to hold out a card while they shot it out of her hand. "Sorry gentlemen but its closing time for the bar."

"Who are you supposed to be?" one of them said.

Ford looked at him sternly. "I'm just a man trying to get some sleep along with the rest of the town. Fun time is over."

"Maybe we don't take orders so well," the drunkest of the two men said.

Ford pulled his gun and hit him on the side of his head. The other man drew his gun, and Ford slapped it out of his hand and slammed his gun across the bridge of his nose. "You're both under arrest."

With a slurred voice one of them said, "For what?"

"I'll give you a whole list of reasons tomorrow. Right now, drop your gun belts; you're both going to jail."

Both men did what Ford said and marched out the door to the jailhouse. He locked them in a cell and gave the key to Gus. "I'll see you in the morning," Ford said and went back to bed.

The next morning, he walked back to the sheriff's office where he was met by Gus and several people of the town who pleaded with him to take the job of sheriff. Their stories of what was happening in the town convinced him to take the job temporarily, until they could get someone permanently. He figured it would be a couple of weeks. After a couple months he came to see that this was an opportunity to do God's work right here in Pleasant Meadows and took the job permanently.

Ray and Logan went to the church the next morning to see the pastor, introduce themselves, and get an idea of where he stood on Biblical teachings.

When he told them he believed the Bible to be the Word of God, they shook his hand and told him they were new in town and would be attending his church. They also said they'd appreciate his prayers.

He informed them his name was Shane Banter and would be honored to pray for them. "I'm pretty new here myself. Been here about two months, and I'd ask for your prayers for me and my work as well,."

In his youth, Reverend Banter had been a skeptic and ridiculer of the Bible, but at twenty he was brought to Christ by a circuit rider named Charles Redman. He experienced a powerful conversion that radically changed his life. Along with salvation, he received a call to serve full time in the ministry.

Ray and Logan walked around town getting to know the layout, stopped at the diner and ate, and then went to their hotel for a good night sleep.

The next day they went to the Sheriff's office. Sheriff Ford was on the walkway anxiously looking down the street toward the saloon. He led them into his office and informed them he'd wired Sheriff Rollins in Dallas and his return wire had only the highest praise for both Ray and Logan.

"I'm happy to inform you both that you have jobs

right here if you want them. Rollins said you were very fast with a gun, Ray, and that you were also very level headed. He said Logan was nearly as fast as you and fast enough to get the job done and also level headed. He said you were both respected and liked by the town's people. Those are two qualities very hard to find in the same person and high praise from a respected sheriff."

"Well, I only hope we can live up to it," Ray said.

Ford looked at them long and hard. "I'm sure you will. Now I have two good, dependable deputies. We're a growing town, and the two of you are Godsends, just what we need in this town. I understand you both walked around town and got acquainted with the layout and met with the reverend. I'm glad you were that interested," Ford said. He kept looking out the window down toward the saloon.

Ray shook Ford's outstretched hand. "All right then, what's our first job?"

Sheriff Ford's face turned grim. "I don't relish doing this," as he threw a wanted poster for Abe Cassie down on his desk.

Ray read what it said. "I've heard of Abe Cassie, most everyone has."

"He's a killer" Ford said, "and his exploits with a gun are legendary."

"What's he wanted for? asked Ray, picking up the wanted poster.

"The last I know, he robbed a bank in Kansas, and one of the customers, a woman eighty years old, didn't respond fast enough so he hit her in the head with the butt of his gun and killed her instantly. He also has 25 notches on his gun. He's the kind of man you pray to God that you never run into."

Ford suddenly jerked the poster out of Ray's hand. "No, on second thought, I can't give you this."

Ray looked stupefied. "Why not?"

"I could never live with myself" Ford said. "No, absolutely not, He may kill you. The truth is I didn't want to face him myself, and sheriff Rollins said how fast you are with a gun. But now I know I have to or I could never live with myself. "

"Where is he?" asked Ray.

Ford cast his eyes to the floor. "Down at the saloon."

Ray took the poster back. "Well I was told that you were a man of your word. You said we have a job and you gave me my first assignment. You can't go back on your word now." Ray spoke matter-of-factly. "He's at the saloon you said?"

"I can't give you this job," said Ford.

Ray stood there with determination on his face. "You didn't. I took it from you."

"I'm the sheriff and I'll face him. He could kill you."

"Then I'll die doing my job. He could kill you too; then the town would have a bunch of deputies with no sheriff to lead them. If for no other reason, I'd be doing it for that old woman. Someone has to care about her."

As Ray walked to the door, Ford could see the determination on his face. Ray spun around. "And besides, I have to make a good impression my first day on the job." With that, Ray returned to Ford's desk, took a badge, and put it on. Then he walked out the door. Sheriff Ford and Logan followed him out and watched him head down the street. It was one of those moments when somber music plays and everyone wonders what's going to happen.

6

Ford was very anxious as he shook his head. "He doesn't know what he's heading into?

Logan put his hand on his shoulder. "He's closer to me than a brother, and I'm not worried. My money is on Ray."

They started down the street. "We have to go down there," Ford said. "If he kills Ray, it's going to fall on us to take down Abe Cassie − or try to."

"If he kills Ray, you and me won't be no match for him," Logan said.

Ford practiced a bit of gallows humor as they stood outside the saloon. "I got to say things sure liven up when you two come to a town."

When Ray entered the saloon, the bartender said, "Is there something I can do for you?"

Ray spoke calmly as he looked around the bar. "I'm here for Abe Cassie, dead or alive." The patrons in the bar fled to the outside door and fled down the street at the sound of that name.

The bartender spoke to Ray with contempt. "Why don't you just get the hell out of here while you still can!"

Abe Cassie was sitting at a table playing cards with two friends. He got up, knocked his chair over behind him, and stood there with a sneer on his face "Well boy, here I am. Now you have me what're you going to do with me?"

Ray threw the poster down at his feet.

Abe Cassie laughed. "You're not very smart are you?"

"You're under arrest," Ray said calmly.

Cassie laughed again and looked at the door. "You're the next notch on my gun if you don't get out of my way."

Ray challenged him, and you could have heard a pin drop. "The only way you're leaving here is by being carried out or by walking over my dead body."

Cassie laughed again. "That can easily be arranged. I would say you really have a problem, don't you?"

Deadly calm came over Ray. "No, you have the problem! You killed an old woman while robbing a bank in Kansas City. You bashed her head in because she didn't move fast enough for you. I'm here to settle that score. My face is the last thing you're ever going to see in this world!"

Abe Cassie went for his gun, but his hand no sooner touched his gun then a bullet ripped into his chest. He went down on his knees and then face down on the filthy floor of the saloon. Ray went over and checked his body, making sure he was dead.

Ray stared at the two men who were playing cards with Cassie. "Are you next?"

Both men shook their heads, stood up with their hands in the air, and started for the door. "You'll never see neither of us again," the shorter one of them said, stopping in front of Ray as if asking permission to leave.

"You're free to go gentlemen. If you decide to come back later, you'll find that this is a town of law and order or you'll be leaving this world the way Abe Cassie did."

"We understand," the other man said.

Ford and Logan had watched it all happen from the side of the saloon and stood with Ray scanning the bar. The trouble was over. Ford nodded to whoever was left in the saloon to leave, and they scampered out like rats leaving a sinking ship.

Outside Ford turned to Ray, "I'm glad you're on my side. I've never seen anyone draw so fast."

Back in the sheriff's office, Ford told his two deputies to go and take Cassie's body to the undertaker. He poured coffee for Ray, Logan, and himself and sat down and looked across at Ray. "Well I have to tell you, you handled that very well. I have to admit, I was rather worried about the outcome of tonight but Logan convinced me you would prevail."

Ray nodded and sipped his coffee. Logan stood up and said, "Well I have to make the rounds." He looked at Ray with a big grin on his face. "Somebody's to do some work around here."

Ray got up from his chair. "Okay, okay, I'll join you. I guess I have to earn my pay."

Logan put his hand on Ray's shoulder, "No, you've done enough for today. Actually I think I'd better contribute something or the boss might think I'm not needed. " He glanced at Sheriff Ford.

Ford smiled. "The fact is you have both convinced me that this is a red banner day for this office. I'll tell you what, in this wild town you have both given me peace of mind." Looking at Ray he said, "You have more than earned your pay today; stay here and finish your coffee, I'll go with Logan and make the rounds. If I don't, pretty soon folks are going to think I'm not necessary around here!"

The next day Ford called them to his office to discuss three items.

First, the bank had notified him that in the last few days one or two men had made trips to the bank, just standing or walking around without doing any business.

Ray and Logan both nodded knowingly before Logan spoke. "This means that these men could have been scouting the bank, sizing it up, taking mental notes, and such with the aim of preparing to rob it."

The second item was that the stagecoach had been held up. And the third was that a few Indians had rustled some cattle from ranches nearby.

Sheriff Ford saw the look in Ray's eyes. "I know, I know, if they're hungry we have to be lenient."

"That's right," Ray said, "My parents would help them out when times were rough, and they always paid us back and helped us out when we were in need. It's a lot easier to deal with them by giving them food than it is to deal with them when they're hungry and desperate for food. We have to remember that they're going to act like we would if our children were hungry."

Sheriff Ford and Logan exchanged looks. Logan had explained to him Ray's friendly dealings with the Indians and their treatment was a sore spot with him.

They could see that Ray wasn't finished and they realized that he had to say something he needed to get off his chest, something he could not hold back:

"They welcomed us when we first came into their territory, until we started forcing them off their own land, killing off the buffalo, and treating them like they were inferior to us. We dreamed up a right to do this that we called Manifest Destiny. He took a deep breath, "Sometimes I think when they go on the warpath that I should join them, for conscience's sake."

He looked down like he thought maybe he'd said too much. Sheriff Ford went to the window and looked out, "No one from this office is going to hassle them, but we can't just stand by and allow them to break the law."

"I understand that," Ray said. "I'm just saying that we can't just go out half-cocked, with our guns blazing, thinking the worst"

Sheriff Ford became very still. "I promise you we'll work with them as much as we can."

Ray relaxed. "Thank you. Look, I didn't mean to imply anything about you. My anger wasn't directed toward you; it came from my past experience. I know you to be a godly and good man. I wasn't implying that you aren't. I'm sorry." Ray said.

"You have nothing to apologize for, I didn't take it personally," Ford said. He went to the door and stopped and turned around. "I think it would be a good idea if I kept my eye on the bank, Logan on the stagecoach, and you check out the cattle rustling".

Ray closed his eyes and nodded his appreciation, "Thank you."

Their plan seemed to be working well. Since sheriff Ford started making regular stops at the bank, the strangers stopped coming. Logan rode shotgun for the stage for the first two days where everyone could see him; then he rode once a week inside the stagecoach on different days so no one could see a pattern.

Ray, as usual, met his problem head on. First, he rode out to the ranches in the area and talked to the owners and foremen whose cattle had been rustled and explained to them that respecting the Indians like equals was much easier than treating them like savages. The buffalo were dying out and each ranch could easily set aside food for the Indians when times were bad, which was not that often.

They were a proud people and would only receive help when really needed, and the Indians would respond by helping the ranchers when needed. Ray said he knew from experience that Indians could be fierce enemies or very reliable friends.

When he was ready to go to the Indian village, sheriff Ford was skeptical about Ray's going alone but agreed with him that if he went there with a group of men there would be trouble. Ford suggested Ray take Logan with him. Ray objected because if he were received as a friend he wouldn't need Logan, and if he were received with hostility it would be better if one man died than two.

Logan argued heatedly that Ray should not go alone. Ray convinced him that if anything happened to him, the sheriff would need Logan. Ray assured them that he would not be harmed if he went in alone.

During the ride there, he spent much time in prayer and recited Scripture from memory. When Ray neared the village, he rode in slowly, careful to show both hands while showing the sign of coming in friendship. Two riders rode out to meet him, one on each side, and escorted him to the chief.

Ray explained that he was there on a "mission of peace and understanding." Then he told the chief of the rustled cattle. The chief suddenly looked around as though expecting an attack. Ray assured him he was not there for revenge and that he was there alone. He said when men are in need they should help each other not harm each other. They needed to cooperate together. The ranchers would give them food when it was needed, and they could respond by helping them when they needed it.

It took some time for him to get his message across with the crude sign language he had worked out with the Arapahos. But slowly the message was delivered. The look on the chief's face as he finally absorbed the message was amazement. He folded his arms and looked very stern at Ray for several minutes to decide whether to believe him or not. Ray showed him the cut on his hand of being a blood brother.

Their eyes met for several minutes. Ray did not dare look away or show any fear. He knew his life weighed in the balance. Finally the chief's eyes softened, and to Ray's surprise he spoke in broken English, "Go in peace with the Great Spirit and His Son who died and rose for us." Tears ran down Ray's eyes as he rode back to town.

Ray felt as though the weight of the world was lifted off of him. He'd been really concerned about this meeting and had prayed hard about it.

That Sunday Ray was asked to teach a Bible class for children. They had asked him to teach adults, but he felt he needed to study more and would start with children. However, he did say a few words after the sermon about his meeting with the Indians and asked for prayer for them. Afterward, they had a church picnic. As he sat there watching the children play their children's games and the adults play horseshoes while discussing the Bible, he thought of his parents. He was comforted by the minister's words at their funerals. He was comforted because he knew from the Bible his words were not simply to comfort him, but true. He began to see this life as a stepping-stone to the next life and was very happy that he would see them again under much better circumstances, and they would never part again.

His study of the Bible and the minister's sermons opened a whole new world for him of the spiritual dimension where Christ was seated at the right hand of the Father as our victorious resurrected Savior. He was thinking of the words of the sermon that morning, about how our victory over death lies in Christ's bloody cross and empty tomb. When Christ went back to heaven, it was as the Conqueror of death for us. As the Representative of all who would believe in Him, when He returned to heaven He left the door open for everyone to follow who confessed Jesus and Savior and Lord.

He was thankful that this life was not all there was. If it were, it wouldn't be much worth living. But Christ made it worth living and has work for us to do. He noticed a new family there from a farm nearby that he had seen in church that morning. They greeted him and shook hands. One of them, a woman carrying a basket, opened it and took out four pies she had baked. She smiled, "My name is Sarah Wakefield and this is my husband James and our two children John and Debbie."

Well that was interesting; she had his mother's name. But that's not all. Ray's meeting with that family would give him an education into slavery that he'd never had before.

7

Sarah's husband, James, was a big man, maybe 6 foot 6 inches and about two hundred and fifty or sixty pounds. Ray could see they were poor from their somewhat ragged clothing. He was drawn to them by their friendliness and simplicity, but mostly by their love for the Lord.

James wore lash marks from being whipped for hiding runaway slaves before Lincoln's emancipation proclamation. He believed the Law of God was above the law of man. The founding father's agreed and wanted to free the slaves but a threatened division among the states prevented it. The fledgling states could not afford a split among them, but needed complete unity as a nation, as war with England, the mightiest nation on earth, was imminent. They felt certain that slavery could not last very long in a nation built on Christian principles. The founders declared that our rights and freedoms came from God who revealed Himself in the Bible, not from a state that could take them away.

The founding fathers established a nation whose rights came from God, not from the government. Therefore, the government couldn't take them away. What the Lord gave, the government could not take away. This was made clear in the birth document of America, The Declaration of Independence was based upon Biblical principles that declared our rights are inalienable because they come from God.

This is why the slaves had to be freed. The Constitution guaranteed the "right to life, liberty, and the pursuit of happiness, without the government's interference. interference.

The Bible was the authority for the founding of America. At the time of the American Revolution, there were about a half million slaves.

The great American black abolitionist, Frederick Douglas, had been a slave in in Maryland who escaped and later became an important spokesman for free blacks in the abolitionist movement. He wrote that the government created by the Constitution "was never in its essence anything but an anti-slavery government. Abolish slavery and no sentence or syllable of the Constitution need be altered," he wrote in 1864.

John Adams, who opposed slavery his whole life, said, "It was a foul contagion in the human character" and "an evil of colossal magnitude." James Madison said it was "the most oppressive dominion ever exercised by man over man."

George Washington wrote: "There is not a man living who wishes more sincerely than I do to see a plan adopted for the abolition of it." While President, he created a plan to rent his land and turn his slaves into paid workers. At the end of his presidency after the death of his wife, he gave them their freedom, while the old and infirm were to be cared for the rest of their lives and their children were to be to learn to read a write and trained in a skill until the age of twenty-five. His estate paid for this care until 1833.

Sadly all citizens were not Christians or even if they were didn't see the evil of slavery. But, back to our story.

James and his son John played horseshoes while Sarah and Debbie cut pieces of pie and passed them out.

Shane Banter, the minister, came over for a piece of pie. He took a bite and closed his eyes and opened them and turning to Sarah he said, "I do not remember ever tasting peach pie this good!"

She smiled, "Good, I'll bring you one every Sunday."

Ray noticed that James Wakefield spoke a lot about Jesus and the Bible with those playing horseshoes. He was very impressed by this man whom the minister said had almost no education but an excellent knowledge of the Bible.

Pastor Banter noticed Ray watching them. He moved closer to Ray, "James wants to learn to be a minister.

"I think with a little polish he will make a good one," Ray said.

"I'm going to teach him as much as I can," Banter said.

"Well, I think he will make a great student, and I can't think of a better teacher. If there is anything I can do, let me know. If you need money or anything, let me know," Ray said.

"I'll let you know, but I definitely want your prayers," Banter answered.

After the church picnic, Ray walked with the Wakefield's to their wagon. He told them that he was glad that James had dedicated his life to the Lord and that if they needed anything to let him know. And if he couldn't help them with it, he would find someone who could.

James thanked Ray and hugged him, almost breaking him in two. The man definitely did not know his own strength. Sarah kissed him on his cheek and said she would bring him a pie every Sunday along with the pastor's pie. Their two children John and Debbie, who were on the wagon, yelled that they loved him and threw him kisses.

For the next three months Pastor Banter worked with James Wakefield, allowing him to give short talks before his sermons and sending him out to visit the sick and older shut-ins. James would read portions of Scripture to them and distribute communion. Many times he would bring Sarah to help clean their homes.

Ray and Logan helped the Wakefields plant their crops in the spring, along with other members of their church. They would round up different jobs for James to do to help earn money. In the winter months, they made sure they got to town for church and had plenty of food and firewood.

After three months, Pastor Banter felt James was ready to preach one Sunday a month and go to camp meetings with the area's circuit rider. Ray was very happy to see that James also had a concern for the Indians.

The town seemed to thrive during this time. The sheriff's office was very peaceful. Crime was way down and the church doubled its membership. Ray decided that it would be a good time to visit his brother Morgan in Abilene. Of course Logan wanted to go along, however sheriff Ford said that would leave him shorthanded. So Logan stayed and Ray went alone.

The trip there was uneventful and gave Ray time to meditate on God's Word, fellowship with God, and pray. The passage of Scripture he chose as his life's promise was Proverbs 3:5-6: "Trust in the Lord with all your heart and lean not on your own understanding; in all your ways acknowledge Him, and He will make your paths straight."

Ray's visit to his brother was for a far more important purpose than a mere visit. His brother Morgan had never given his life to Christ. His mom and dad had made the life changing decision to trust Christ as Ray had done recently. But Morgan had always talked around the subject with Christian language but without its real meaning.

When Ray arrived, Morgan was sitting on their porch with His wife Rachel, smoking his pipe while their two children, Tom and Beth, played in the front yard. When Ray was close enough to be recognized, Morgan jumped up and ran to meet him. "Welcome to my humble home. You must be hungry and tired."

Rachel welcomed him with a hug. "I'll make you something to eat," she said.

"And some coffee," Morgan added.

Ray shook his head back and forth. "Now don't be making a big fuss."

"No fuss at all," Morgan said. "We have lots to talk about."

After Ray ate, they talked for a while. Then Rachel went to bed and Morgan lit his pipe. After a few minutes Morgan said, "So what brings you here, sheriff business?"

"No, I'm here for two reasons. I wanted to see my older brother…" Ray hesitated a moment. "…and I wanted to talk to you about the Lord."

Morgan frowned. "What are you talking about? I make sure Rachel and the kids go to church regularly and sometimes I go myself."

Ray got real serious. "I'm not talking about just going to church. You know, mom and dad enjoyed talking about the Lord and reading the Bible and having devotions, as I do now, but you always seemed to separate yourself."

Morgan started cleaning his pipe. "All right, maybe I don't believe the same way you do."

Ray quietly said, "And what way do you believe?"

Morgan looked like he felt trapped. "I didn't want to go into all this, but you seem to insist that I do. All right, you brought up about you, Mom, and Dad being so caught up with God. So where are Mom and Dad for all their religion? They're dead, murdered, senselessly murdered, and you're on the run. And let's not forget that me and Rachel once had three children but now have only two because our little girl, who was only seven at the time, was bit by a rattle snake and died. So where was God then?" Tears started running down his face. Ray could feel Morgan's anger and hurt and the depth of his emotion.

Morgan continued. "I just don't think I can serve a God who lets His people go through all this misery while He just sits and watches from His heavenly throne. There I said it. Are you happy now?" Morgan threw his pipe across the room.

Ray looked down and shook his head. He got up, walked over and picked up the pipe, and set it on the table. Then he sat down next to Morgan who had tears in his eyes. "God doesn't just sit there and watch our suffering. He got off His throne and took upon Himself humanity in order to suffer and die for our sins. Do you get that? HE suffered for the sins WE committed against HIM."

Ray continued. "God is holy, and He is love. His holiness demands that our sins be judged and paid for, which can't happen by anything we do or say, even going to church on Sundays and being a good person.

God's love carried this judgment out on Himself, in the Person of His Son. He can promise a restored relationship to all those who call upon the name of Jesus in faith and repentance.

Jesus told us very plainly in John 16:33 that "In this world you will have trouble. But take heart! I have overcome the world." That means we will face troubles and trials, but He will face them with us.

Morgan was weeping freely now. "It hurts," he said.

Ray put his arm around his brother's shoulder. "I know it does. God is not a faraway onlooker of our sorrows; He has entered into our sorrows and misery right there with us. He calls us to trust Him and promises to make everything all right. But until that happens, we are to trust Him and do everything we can to tell others about Him and help alleviate suffering as best we can."

Ray took out a Bible he had brought and held it up. "On the authority of this book, I can tell you that your little girl, Rebecca, is not really dead. She is with Jesus and her body here on earth is only sleeping, to be resurrected when Christ comes again. You will see her again if you trust in Jesus as she did."

Morgan's eyes widened as though ice water had been thrown in his face. Then his eyes softened. For the first time, he let the reality of what Ray said sink in.

Morgan hung his head. "I don't know what to say. I never really grasped that before. I haven't seen God in the right way. Now I see why you came here."

That night Ray and Morgan read through some Bible verses and prayed that God would reveal the truth of them to Morgan. Ray asked Morgan if he truly believed that Jesus Christ died for his sins and rose again as Savior and Lord. Morgan shook his head with tears in his eyes. "Yes," he said. "I believe that with all my heart".

Ray spoke with conviction. "On the authority of God's Word, I can tell you that you have passed from death into life and are now a new creation in Christ Jesus. You are a child of God based solely on what Jesus Christ did on your behalf."

They both laughed and hugged and went through more Bible verses on living the Christian life. "For the first time I feel like a child of God," Morgan said.

"That's great," his brother said, "but always remember that the reality of salvation is not based on your feelings but on the unmovable Word of God."

The next morning Morgan told Rachel what had happened after she went to bed. He told her that they needed to have Bible studies and prayer together with the children and all of them attend church together as a family.

Rachel's eyes welled up with tears as she hugged

Morgan. She looked at Ray over Morgan's shoulder and silently mouthed the words, "Thank you."

Rachel made a breakfast like at a wedding feast and packed some food for Ray to eat on the way back. They walked Ray out to his horse. Morgan gave Ray a hug. "Thanks for coming; thanks for caring," he said. "So where are you headed from here?"

"Back home," Ray said. "You have a good church and a good pastor. I had a long talk with him after Mom and Dad's funerals. He's a good man. Get to know him; help him out at the church; have him over often for meals."

"We'll do that," Rachel said. Morgan hugged him again. "Come more often," Rachel pleaded.

"I will" Ray said. "I'll have to bring Logan sometime."

"He's always welcome," Morgan said. As Ray rode off he was thankful to God for how things turned out. But his trip wasn't over quite yet.

8

A few miles from down the road, Ray passed a clump of trees and a pond of water. He saw a figure on the ground and rode over. A man was clearly in agony and lay there moaning with his eyes closed. Ray got off his horse. The man opened his eyes as Ray approached. "Oh, thank God, "he said. "My horse threw me when we came upon a rattler."

"How bad are you hurt?" Ray asked, kneeling down beside him.

"I think my back is broke. I can't move my legs or my head, only my arms. Could you please give me some water."

Ray reached for his canteen and helped him drink. "Where are you from and where were you headed?"

"It doesn't matter; I'm finished. I'll make you a deal," he said through clenched teeth. "You help me and I'll help you."

"I don't follow you. How can you help me?" Ray asked.

"I came with three other men who work for Prescott Monahan. Monahan planted a man in your town to spy on you. When he sent word that you left on a trip to visit your brother, he sent us to meet you, but I got separated from the others and here I lay.

"Where are they?" Ray asked.

"I honestly don't know. Like I said, we got separated, but they're out there. I helped you; now please help me."

Ray kind of knew what the man wanted done but asked anyway. "What do you want me to do for you?"

"I can use my hands but I can't reach my gun," he said. "I need you to either put a bullet in my head or hand me my gun so I can do it." He got all the words out with much effort.

"Have you made peace with God?" Ray asked.

"The best I know how. Can you help me? Please, I'm afraid."

Ray quoted John 3:16-18 from memory: "For God so loved the world that He gave His one and only Son, that whosoever believes in Him shall not perish but have eternal life. For God did not send His Son into the world to condemn the world, but to save the world through Him. Whoever believes in Him is not condemned, but whoever does not believe stands condemned already because he has not believed in the name of God's one and only Son."

Ray asked the dying man if he confessed that he was a sinner and believed that Jesus took the judgment that he deserved. He said yes. Ray quoted Scripture giving him assurance of his relationship to God through Christ: "Therefore, there is now no condemnation for those who are in Christ Jesus" (Romans 8:1).

Then Ray reached down and pulled his gun out of his holster. "Wait," the man said. "In my pocket is a thousand dollar gold piece. Take it. It's the money Monahan paid each of us to kill you."

Ray took the money, handed him his gun, and turned his back. A shot rang out.

Ray wished he could bury him but had no shovel. The scavengers would soon take care of the body. He filled his canteen in the pond nearby and rode toward home, aware that he would probably meet the other three men working for Prescott Monahan sooner or later. If he paid four men a thousand dollars each, he must want revenge badly.

After riding half a day more, he stopped and ate some of the food that Rachel had packed for him. Then it began to rain. The gentle rain felt good as he got back on his horse, but suddenly it began to pour. He rode in the drenching rain until he came to some foothills with a cave and some boulders. He got off his horse and sought shelter behind a boulder. A short distance away, he could see three men on a ridge. He couldn't believe his luck. It was Monahan's men. They hadn't seen him.

He tied his horse to a bush and quickly made his way around behind them. But he had the bad luck of spooking their horses, alerting them that he was there. They turned around and quickly slumped down.

"Gentlemen, your fourth member is dead, and I have your horses, so I think it would be in your interest to talk."

"All right, so talk," one of them said.

"Throw down your guns, and I will give you your horses back," Ray said.

"If we throw our guns down Monahan will have us all killed."

Ray spoke matter-of-factly. "If you don't throw your guns down, I'm going to kill you right here. It's up to you."

"If we throw down our guns, how do we know you'll keep your end of the bargain?"

"Look, I have no desire to have a shoot-out with three men." Ray could see them talking to each other while they were talking to him. He felt they were stalling and at the right time they would all come out shooting.

One of the men spoke up. "Give us our horses and you can ride out of here."

Ray knew it was a trap, but he wanted to finish this thing off. He knew he couldn't trust them. If he did ride out of there, he knew they'd still by laying for him.

Monahan was a very wealthy man and was used to getting what he wanted, and what he wanted was revenge for his son's hanging. So Ray decided to take the gamble of an ambush after giving back their horses. He felt he stood a good chance against them.

Ray yelled back at them. "All right, you have a deal." He waited by the horses as the three men came out in the open. Ray felt the tension building as he realized that a split-second would mean the difference between life and death. He felt a peaceful calm come over him. In a moment it was over. Ray fired three deadly shots and three men hit the ground. One of the three dropped to his knees, fatally wounded; but before he died, he fired and hit Ray in the chest. The impact knocked him to the ground. Ray gasped for air as he lay there.

He wondered how badly he was hurt. He could feel that it was close to his heart. He breathed a prayer, "Lord, I'm in your hands, live or die." He felt his chest with his right hand; he could not lift his left hand. His chest was numb. He felt around and felt something hard and jagged, which he realized was his deputy's badge. He tore it off his shirt. It was badly bent but no blood on it.

He felt no wound or hole in his chest. It gradually dawned on him that the bullet had hit his badge, and he may only have a broken rib. He lay there until he got his bearings, wondering if he could get on his horse. He dizzily struggled to his feet and agonized trying to get on his horse. After three attempts he finally made it. He slumped forward and let his horse bring him home.

It was near dark when his horse stopped in front of the sheriff's office. Sheriff Ford and a deputy were sitting on the walkway. They helped Ray off his horse and brought him into the office. Logan was making the rounds. They brought Ray into the back room and lay him on the bed. Sheriff Ford told Pat, one of his deputies, to bring the doctor from next door.

Logan had just finished his rounds when the doctor came. Sheriff Ford introduced Ray and Doc Rayburn. After the doctor looked Ray over, he asked Pat to come with him to his office and help him get some things he needed.

Once back, the doctor made a bandage with healing ointments and put it on Ray's chest. He told Ray to get lots of rest and use his left arm as little as possible for the next three or four days.

Logan was waiting in the other room and talked to the doctor as he was leaving. "How is Ray. How badly was he hurt?"

"He's very lucky to be alive, but he'll be all right in a few days with the bandage and some rest. He has a bruised rib and will need some time to get back to his normal activities. That rib is going to be sore for several days and cause him to be short of breath with any exertion. Right now, his body's in shock. By tomorrow it will wear off and he'll be in a lot more pain."

When the doctor left, Logan went into Ray's room. Ray appeared to be sleeping but opened his eyes when Logan approached.

Logan shook his head and kidded Ray. "I just can't trust you out of my sight. I told you to take me with you. You'll do most anything to get out of work won't you? Now you get to lay around while I do all the work, as usual." Logan laughed heartily at his own humor. "I've been given strict orders not to let you exert yourself, which means I'll have to do everything for you. You better not give me any trouble!"

"Yes Mommy, I'll be good," Ray said and closed his eyes and went to sleep.

The next morning Ray told the sheriff and Logan about the three men sent from Prescott Monahan. He told them where to find them.

"They ambushed me, and I had no choice but to kill

them. Oh, by the way, there is a thousand dollar gold-piece on each of them, payment from Monahan to kill me. The money's not going to do them any good. Besides, I earned it. There are a lot of places we can give that money, and we sure ain't going to give it back to Monahan."

The sheriff told Logan to handle it. "I'll get on it right away," Logan said and turned to Ray as he was going out the door. "One of the deputies will take care of anything you need. He's making you breakfast now."

"Wait," Ray said. "Their three horses are somewhere back there. I was in no shape to bring them back."

The sheriff stepped toward Logan. "Better take a deputy with you."

Logan was back to his humorous and kidding self. "Well, you know, you send a boy to do a man's job and this is what you get. As usual I have to go and clean up your mess, Ray."

As Logan was going out the door, Ray turned serious. "Hey, Logan, I should have taken you with me."

Logan smiled. "You did pretty damn good on your own. Pray for me." Then he went out the door.

Later, the sheriff came back with Doc Rayburn to change Ray's bandage, who expressed his concern for Logan. The sheriff said he sent two deputies with him. "He'll be all right. He's smart. He'll get the job done."

That cheered Ray up. The doctor said he felt good about Ray's injury. "Just don't exert yourself too much."

Ray asked the sheriff to help him go outside and sit on the walkway. "If you can make it," Ford said, "but like the doctor said, don't exert yourself too much."

Ray tried standing up and sat right back down. "Give me your right arm," the sheriff said.

"Today is when you are going to really feel it," Doc Rayburn said. "You should be thankful you were wearing that badge."

Ray stood up with the sheriff holding his right

arm, just as Pastor Banter came in the door. The pastor held the door open for them to go out and followed them and sat down next to Ray on the walkway. "So how are you feeling?"

"I've been better," Ray said, "but I really should be dead you know."

"I know," the pastor said. "I think God has a plan for you. What are the odds of that bullet hitting that little badge by coincidence?"

"I was thinking that myself," Sheriff Ford said.

Some minutes later, the deputy helped Ray back inside where he spent most of the day sleeping and reading the Bible. The deputy made sure he ate some of the healthy stew he had made and some pie Sarah Wakefield had brought while he was sleeping. Ray expressed regret that He missed seeing her and her husband James. The deputy assured him they would be back later.

Ray was anxious for Logan to return. He figured at least two days to round up the horses. He figured there might be a good chance that somebody would find those horses and claim them. That was all right with him as long as they were taken care of. His fear was that Logan might unexpectedly run into more of Monahan's men.

Later Sarah and James Wakefield came back to visit Ray. James had some Bible questions he wanted to ask him. Deputy Dale brought them coffee. Ray sat up and took a sip. "I'm glad you're going deeper into the study of the Bible and have questions to ask me." He took another sip of coffee. "Ask away."

This was his first question. "If a person is saved from all their sins and Christ's righteousness is given to them, then why don't God just take us up to heaven right then. Wouldn't that save us all a lot of heartaches?"

"God leaves us here to win others to Christ who would not have been won had God taken us to be with Him. One thing the Bible is very clear about is that we are saved to serve. Jesus' call to us is 'Follow Me and I will make you fishers of men.' This means a life of service, and a life of service means a life Bible study and prayer."

"All right, but how do you know God's will for your life?"

"He will lead you as you study the Word and pray. Just keep doing what you're doing and you'll be fine," Ray answered.

"But then why do believers have to appear before the Judgment Seat of Christ, if all our sins are already forgiven?" Sarah asked.

James patted her on the back, "Good question!"

"That's a good question and one that's asked a lot. The answer is that the Judgment Seat of Christ is not a judgment concerning salvation, which has already taken place for believers in Christ when they are born-again.

Ray took out his Bible and turned to the 3rd chapter of John and read verses 16-18. "Here is what Jesus said on this subject: 'For God so loved the world that He gave His one and only Son, that whoever believes in him shall not perish but have eternal life. For God did not send His Son into the world to condemn the world, but to save the world through him. Whoever believes in him is not condemned, but whoever does not believe stands condemned already because he has not believed in the name of God's one and only Son.'

"Jesus continues in verse 38: 'Whoever believes in the Son has eternal life, but whoever rejects the Son will not see life, for God's wrath remains on him.'

"And finally, in John 5:24 Jesus says: 'I tell you the truth, whoever hears my word and believes Him who sent me has eternal life and will not be condemned, he has crossed over from death to life.'

"So, we see that as far as salvation is concerned, the believer in Christ has already been judged and has received eternal life through faith in Christ. Our faith does not earn salvation. It cannot be earned; it is a free gift from God based solely on what Christ did for us. But like all gifts, it must be received, and this is done by simply taking God at His word and putting your eternal destiny into His hands simply because He asks you to. The Judgment Seat of Christ is for rewards for service after the believer has received Christ. Salvation is through faith alone, but rewards are for service after salvation. God makes it very clear that He will not accept our good works as payment for salvation.

It is an offense to a holy God to reject what Christ did on our behalf and think we can earn it by our good works. If salvation could be earned, Christ would not have had to suffer and die in our behalf. But after we have received salvation as a free gift provided by Christ alone, God will receive our good works not as payment for our sins but done out of gratitude for our salvation provided by God through Jesus Christ. And not only will He accept our good works, but He will reward us for them. This is the purpose of The Judgment Seat of Christ."

For another hour, James and Sarah Wakefield asked questions about the Bible and Ray answered them as best he could.

After the Wakefields left, a man ran into the sheriff's office and told him there was a fight at the saloon. Ford called out to his two deputies, and Pat, who was cleaning out the jailcells, motioned to Dale, the deputy caring for Ray, to stay and he would take care of the matter.

Ford said, "There's trouble down there at the saloon, and I want you to go and check it out." Lately he'd been giving his deputies more responsibilities.

Ford watched nervously as Pat walked down to the saloon. He really missed Ray's and Logan's help. Ford watched until Pat came out with two men he had arrested and brought them to the jail and locked them up.

Back out on the walkway he told the sheriff, "They will be no problem; they're just drunk and need to sleep it off."

"Good job," Ford said. "You handled that nicely." He had been teaching his deputies to use just the right force to get the job done.

Over the next few days, Ray healed rapidly. Logan returned after four days with a successful story to tell. He recovered all the horses and found them good homes. Monahan's men did not return. And he recovered the three one thousand dollar gold coins. Logan set the coins down on the small table beside Ray's bed. "Here's the coins you earned. I know you have a good use for them."

"I definitely do, the first thing I want to do is give you one of them; you earned it." Logan was pleased and thankful.

Later Ray brought the two other gold pieces to the bank and cashed them in for smaller currency. When Sarah and James Wakefield visited again, he gave them $500 to help them out while James spent his time learning the ministry. James had told Reverend Banter that he felt he might do more good as a circuit rider. Banter said he agreed but wanted him to know the dangerous and difficult demands of a circuit rider.

Before not too long, Ray was back to work, gradually taking on more responsibilities as he grew stronger. One day in the early afternoon, Ray met Dwight Braxton outside the general store. Dwight was one of three famous and feared outlaw brothers fast with a gun. Ray felt he had to confront him.

Ray spoke with due respect. He knew men like him didn't like to be pushed around or showed disrespect.

"I'm a deputy here and I'm not pushing for trouble, but you and your two brothers are well known for trouble. I don't care what you did in the past; but this is a peaceful town, and I expect you to keep it that way."

Dwight studied him for a few moments. "I'm not here for any trouble; I'm here alone. My brothers may come later ,but there will be no trouble from any of us. To tell you the truth, we're all trying to get away from that life."

"I can appreciate that," Ray said. "I haven't always been a law man and I can understand where you're coming from."

"I'm staying at the hotel and working out at the Henderson ranch. So I'll be seeing you around," Dwight said.

Ray smiled and shook his hand. "Nice meeting you."

Dwight nodded, mounted his horse, and left. Ray finished making his rounds, though he felt very tired and sore. Back in the sheriff's office, he sat down at the table exhausted. Sheriff Ford poured him a cup of coffee and told him to take the rest of the day off.

Ford sat down next to Ray. "I saw you talking to one of the Braxton brothers. What was that about?"

Ray took a sip of his coffee, "I Just wanted to tell him that this is a peaceful town and I expected him to help keep it that way. He said he was here alone and his brothers may come later, and that he wasn't here to cause trouble and neither would his brothers. He said he wanted to leave his old life. He's staying in town at the hotel and working at the Henderson ranch." He took another sip of coffee, "I believe him. He seems to be in the situation I've been in."

"I hope you're right," Ford said. "The Braxton brothers are a very formidable and dangerous trio to be together in the same town. Ray went to bed and slept the rest of the day.

The three Braxton brothers, Dwight, John, and Robert (Bob), were orphaned at an early age. They were born about a year apart. They were all too young but managed to join in the Civil War on the Northern side. They were never the same after that. They entered the war as innocent young men who had no home life and the Army gave them a place to belong. But the things they saw changed them into hardened and bitter young men, quick tempered and easily set off.

Fresh out of the army and angry at man's inhumanity to man, they gravitated to lives of crime. They became legendary as fast guns with violent tempers. But after years of this lifestyle, they grew weary of it. John and Bob got jobs breaking wild stallions. Dwight was brought to Christ through a Circuit Rider and went to Pleasant Meadows to collect his thoughts and get his bearings.

9

Ray healed up over the next several days.

One afternoon, seven men rode into town. Ford's experienced eye told him that these were not cattlemen or men from one of the ranches coming in for supplies. These were serious men here to take care of business. Sheriff Ford and Logan watched them from the walkway.

Four of the men went into the saloon, and three walked to the bank, two of which went inside. Sheriff Ford told Logan to get Ray. "It looks like a hit on the bank. Those two are scouting the bank while the others, at the saloon, are waiting for their cue. They plan to hit quickly and ride out before the town knows what happened."

Ford noticed that none of the seven were any of the Braxton Brothers. He was greatly relieved because they were known for their fast guns and ruthlessness. He had been suspicious at first because of Dwight Braxton being in town. He was aware that Dwight was in the hotel across the street next to the saloon that the other four men had entered. He told deputies Pat and Dale to stick around; there may be trouble. Dwight Braxton came out of the hotel and looked down the street to where sheriff Ford and his deputies were.

Logan returned with Ray, and Braxton started walking toward them. Ford held his breath with his eyes focused on Braxton, trying to figure out what this meant. As Braxton approached, Ray stepped out to meet him.

Ford sent his two deputies, Pat and Dale, to the bank.

Braxton looking around walked up to Ray. "I'm no dummy. I can see what's going on; you have a bank robbery going down."

"And where do you stand?" Ray asked.

Braxton looked down the street toward the bank. "I told you before I ain't here for trouble. I want out of that life," He threw his hands up. "I'm offering my help. If you don't want it, I'll just go on back to my hotel room."

Ray looked over at Ford and Logan and nodded to them that Braxton was okay. "We're in no position to turn down help."

"That's for sure. Those are some pretty tough and desperate looking men."

The man outside the bank walked down toward the saloon and gave a signal to the man outside of it. Ford was sure that this was their cue. That outside-the-saloon man signaled to those inside to come outside. Then, the four of them got on their horses and rode down to the bank and waited outside.

Ford and his men started walking over to the bank. "This is it," Ford said, as they spread out on both sides of the street. The men outside the bank waited and watched. Just then the two men inside the bank came out holding bags of money.

Pat and Dale, who were hiding nearby, stepped out and started shooting. Both men fell, dropping the bags of money. Two men on horseback jumped down and grabbed the bags. Dale was hit and fell holding his stomach. Logan, holding a shotgun, brought down the third man, but he was hit in the hip. Ford, Ray, and Braxton fired on the four men on horseback, bringing all four down.

In the fierce gun battle on the streets of Pleasant Meadows, Ford was severely wounded in the chest and Ray was hit in the shoulder.

As quickly as it had started, it was over and the action shifted to tending to the wounded. Citizens came out to help, bringing a wagon on which they quickly put Ford and Dale, both of whom were critically wounded, Logan who couldn't walk, and Ray. Another wagon was brought for the outlaws, four of whom were dead. Braxton and Pat, who were not wounded, helped put the dead bodies on a that wagon, which was driven to the undertaker. The first wagon was driven to the doctor's office.

Doc Rayburn was mainly worried about Ford, Dale, and one of the outlaws. Sadly, Dale died on the way to the doctor's office, and the outlaw died before he could be treated. The main concern was for Ford's chest wound. The doc worked to get him stable and stayed in the back room watching him all night. Braxton and Pat kept watch on Ray and Logan.

The two outlaws not seriously wounded were locked in cells. Though in serious condition, Sheriff Ford expressed concern that more of the outlaw gang might ride in or other trouble would happen, since only Braxton and Pat were available to handle anything. He was anxious to deputize Braxton, who was more than willing to serve in that capacity. He was thankful that in such a bloody shootout no citizens were harmed.

The next morning, the first thing the doctor did was change Ford's and Logan's bandages. Then he changed Ray's shoulder bandage.

Ford, while laying in bed, had Braxton stand before him, with his hand on a Bible, and deputized him.

Braxton shook his head and grinned. "Can you believe I'm a lawman?" he said to Ray.

Ray laughed. "Well you said you wanted to get out of that old life. You can't get more away from that life than this.

"You were definitely a God send," Sheriff Ford said.

"It's funny how things work out isn't it," Ray commented.

Braxton and Pat made the rounds while Ray, whose wound was in the left shoulder, helped around the jailhouse. Logan was anxious to help, but his hip wound kept him off his feet.

Pastor Banter ministered to all of them and the outlaws in the cell, reading the Bible and praying. He had good news for Ray from Pastor Mills. His brother Morgan had taken Ray's advice and got involved in Reverend Mill's church and was helping him reach their town for Christ.

James Wakefield helped out, and to everyone's delight Sarah served some of her famous pie. Braxton and Pat returned in time for pie and then sat out on the walkway watching over the town. Many of the town's people came by to bring homemade goodies and help out in any way they could.

Ray's injuries healed up over the next couple of months. He was given jobs that he could handle as he improved. He took some time to talk to pastor Banter about the Wakefields and their desire to serve the Lord. Banter said that James was thinking that maybe rather than a pastor's life, God was calling him to the hard life of a circuit rider, but he was worried about his wife Sarah while James was gone.

Ray was thrilled that James wanted to be a circuit rider. He talked it over with Logan, and they decided to help provide and care for Sarah. She could work at the church and help at the diner and the hotel. Sheriff Ford said he could use her help around his office, with Dale having died. She could help around when Pat was making his rounds at night and, of course, bake her pies. She could stay at the hotel for free and teach Sunday school and the Bible to the women of the church. Braxton and Logan would help maintain the Wakefields' cabin and property. Ray gave that news to pastor Banter and James Wakefield, who were beyond thankful.

Ray was beginning to see that God did have a plan for his life, but he did feel trapped. He was on the run for killing those cattlemen and Jack Garth. If he turned himself in, he'd be hanged. He dedicated himself to God to lead and guide him.

Ray still had the $2,500 from the gold pieces. He would use that for the Lord's work, since he was earning pay from his deputy's job.

Ray heard great news from his brother Morgan that he was helping his pastor at church and leading camp meetings to reach many for Christ. And it was a great comfort to Ray to see Logan grow in his knowledge of the Lord and leading many of the town's people to the Lord. He wasn't sure of the end game for himself, but he wanted his life to count for God, and he wanted to leave something behind to carry on his work for Him.

Ray felt it was time to visit Dallas and see Amber Marie and Sheriff Rollins. Recently Ford had hired three more deputies, and Ray felt it was a good time to leave while Ford could spare him for a couple of weeks. He had been gone from Dalas for two years and was amazed at how fast time had gone by.

Contact with Amber would be hard because, later on, it would make him more aware of her absence. Being on the run and not knowing when his time would run out made life very hard to plan on a marriage. He'd always be looking over his shoulder for someone to take him out, and he had some important things he felt he needed to do before then.

Before going, Ray stopped at the church and gave pastor Banter a thousand dollars for his church work and for James Wakefield to begin his ministry as a circuit rider and to care for his wife, Sarah. Pastor Banter gave Ray a new Bible because his was getting quite worn. They both knelt down and prayed together.

Ray went to see Sheriff Ford and said he'd be back

in a few weeks. Logan said he thought it would be a good idea if he went, what with the Sheriff having plenty of help, its being a long trip, and not knowing what trouble may lay before Ray.

Ray agreed that his company would be appreciated. Ray, Logan, and Ford prayed together. The two buddies would get a good night's sleep and leave in the morning.

The next morning as the sun rose in the east, they packed their saddlebags, said goodbye to everyone, and started on their journey.

The trip was blistering hot and slow for the first several hours until they came to an area that was a hangout for men wanted by the law. They found a place in the shade and rested during the hottest part of the day, figuring to ride again in the cool of the evening and night. They were on alert because wherever men who were wanted by the law were gathered, there would sooner or later be bounty hunters. In the world of outlaws and bounty hunters, you'd find some of the toughest and meanest men alive.

When they were ready to travel, they noticed three men watching them. One of them was drinking whiskey from a bottle kept in his saddlebag, and he passed it around to his friends. Ray nudged Logan and said, "I can see that it's time to move on."

"I guess so," Logan responded.

One of the men said something to the other two and they all had a laugh. Ray and Logan mounted their horses and slowly rode past them.

They rode on under the starry sky until they reached a town near Dallas. There they rented a room for the night, watered their horses, and bought two bags of oats for their stabled horses.

In the morning they ate at the diner and filled their canteens. On the way to the stable, they were closely watched by two men who Ray's experienced eye told him were bounty hunters.

Sure enough when Ray and Logan came out leading their horses, they were met by the two men. But to Ray's total surprise, it was Logan they confronted. They mistook him for someone else. "You James Dutton?" one of them with pearl-handled guns asked.

Logan shook his head. "Guys, you have me mixed up with someone else; I am not this James Dutton," he said while looking over at Ray. The other bounty hunter shoved Logan and snapped, "Don't look at him. He's not going to help you!"

Ray could see that they liked to throw their weight around and impress people with their authority and intimidate them. Those were the kind of men Ray didn't like.

Ray stepped away from his horse out in the open, facing both men. "You're wrong about that. He's obviously the wrong man. You should be more careful. But I'll tell you what, since you're looking for trouble, you found it. There's a bounty out on me. I'm the one you should want. My name's Ray Williams. If you want to take me, make a move."

The blood drained from both of their faces. They looked at each other and both shook their heads and held up their hands. They wanted no part of Ray Williams. "Look," one of them said. "We did jump too fast on your friend here, and we want no part of you Mister Williams. We're not insane!"

Ray shot back. "No you just want to be big shots and throw your weight around no matter who it hurts. Ray could see that they were just two young boys wanting glory without earning it, simply by killing another man. Ray decided to teach them a lesson, hopefully in time to save their lives.

"It's a little too late to back down now," Ray said. "You were pushing for a gun fight and now you have one.

There is only one way a gun fight ends and that's when someone dies."

"You can't just shoot us down," the one with the pearl-handled guns said.

"I'm not just shooting you down, I'm letting you draw, either one at a time or both together, it doesn't matter to me."

The young man started begging. "Please, we made a mistake and we're sorry."

The other man joined in. "Just let us go. We have families, we're sorry." He started sobbing.

"You should have thought of that before. Two big shots like you shouldn't have any trouble taking a simple outlaw like me in," Ray said. He looked at Logan, "Let's go." They mounted their horses and rode away to the great relief of the two very frightened bounty hunters.

News soon spread that Ray Williams was in the area. By the time they arrived in Dallas, Ray and Logan were watching everywhere for lawmen and bounty hunters. When they arrived in the town of Cool Waters, Ray wondered if there could ever be a future for him. When they arrived at Sheriff Rollins' office, there was a happy reunion. Roger and Don Travis, the former Texas Rangers who were now deputies for Rollins, greeted them.

Rollins hugged Ray with tears in his eyes. Then he grabbed Logan. "I knew you'd bring him back if we sent you with him."

"How is Amber doing?" Ray asked. He felt a bitter sweetness of love for her but actually hoped she had found someone else. He loved her too much to bring her into his way of life. It was never about him but always about her and her happiness.

Rollins told him she was at a church social with Bill Eastman. "Don't worry," he said, "it's not anything serious, just friendship and working together for the Lord. Her heart is completely yours." Ray smiled and breathed a prayer that God would work things out.

"How long you going to be here?" Rollins asked Logan.

Logan pointed at Ray. "That's up to him."

Ray didn't want to run into any trouble while he was there visiting with Amber and her father. "For a couple of days," Ray said. Logan shot him a very surprised look. "We're needed back in Pleasant Meadows, and we have to be back soon." He felt that trapped, hopeless, feeling again.

"I'll bet you guys are starved," Rollins said and took them over to the diner in the backroom of the saloon. He bought each of them a steak dinner. From there, they went to the church social.

Amber wept when she saw Ray. Bill Eastman clearly felt out of place, but Ray made him feel welcome and insisted on meeting him. When Amber went in to discuss things with the minister, Ray had a talk with Bill Eastman. He found out that he was a believer in Christ, and it wasn't hard to see that he liked Amber more than just as a friend. But he was very respectful toward Ray and her feelings for him.

After two days, Ray felt fortunate that no lawman or bounty hunter had confronted him. Amber was disappointed that he was leaving so soon. He was more convinced than ever that this was no life for the woman he loved. Ray, to Amber's surprise, told her that he was very impressed with Bill Eastman.

Ray next went to Rollins' office. Ray embraced Rollins and told him that it was impossible for Amber and him to have a life together and that he hoped she would meet someone like Bill Eastman.

Rollins stared at him for several moments and then with a pained look on his face nodded that he understood what Ray was telling him. Outside, after mounting his horse, he was handed an envelope by Amber that said,

"To my dearest love," and a Bible signed by her. Ray struggled to hold back tears.

After riding out of town, Ray read the letter and broke down and wept uncontrollably. Logan asked if he was all right. Ray wiped away the tears and took a deep breath and his face showed his resignation to a will above his and gave Amber up to God. Then Ray and Logan started back to Pleasant Meadows. Ray was very thankful for Logan's friendship, especially at a time like this.

The ride back to Oklahoma was sad and quiet. They avoided any towns or big ranches that might draw bounty hunters or lawmen. When they neared Pleasant Meadows, they thought they could relax. That thought was soon dispelled.

As they came around a bend in the road with hills and trees all around, they were ambushed from two directions. Jumping off their horses, they took cover among the trees. Ray had been nicked in his neck. The gunfire came from both sides of the road. Both men lay on their stomachs with their guns out, waiting.

Ray crawled over to a tree and sat up with his back against it, blood flowing from his neck. Logan stood up and walked over to him. "Are you all right?" As he looked at the wound, he realized it was worse than he had first thought.

"I'm all right. I sure wish people would quit shooting at me!" It was an odd time for such humor. Both men froze as they heard someone walking on dry leaves. They could hear their own hearts beating as the steps came closer. Ray stood up next to Logan.

It was hard to tell how many; they only knew that there were at least two. Suddenly, three men came out in the open. Ray and Logan both fired, each hitting one. Logan grabbed Ray and held him down and covered him with his own body. The third gunman fired, hitting Logan in the back. Ray fired three bullets into the man, whom he recognized as one of Prescott Monahan's men.

Ray was badly shaken as Logan's limp body slumped to the ground, his eyes looking into Ray's. Ray realized he was still breathing as he lay groaning in pain. Ray had to control his emotions and think clearly. He knew he was within an hour's ride from town. He had to leave Logan and ride to town and get help and come back for him.

He had to hurry – Logan's life depended on it. He took one of his saddlebags and made a pillow for Logan. He knelt down and said, "Hang on, please hang on, I'll be back for you soon." Ray mounted his horse, breathed a prayer, and made the ride of his life for the five miles that separated him from Pleasant Meadows.

When he arrived at the sheriff's office, Sheriff Ford was on the walkway. Ray talked as if he were out of breath. "We were ambushed by Prescott Manahan's men. Logan's been shot. He's hurt too seriously to be moved, so I had to leave him and come back for help. We have to go back with a wagon and get him."

"How bad is he hurt?" Ford asked. Braxton and Pat came out of the sheriff's office, and Braxton hurried off to fetch the doctor. "He was shot in the back at close range," Ray said between sobs.

"Oh God!" Ford said. "You two go with him and hurry. Hurry!" he said again, pointing at Braxton and Pat. Pat ran back into the Sheriff's office and grabbed the thin mattress covering his bed and threw it on the wagon outside the sheriff's office. Braxton helped the doctor onto the wagon. Ray drove the wagon, and off they all went.

Ray drove the wagon as if he were in a race, which, in a way he was, the race for Logan's life. They crossed the five miles in the blink of an eye. When they arrived Ray jumped off the wagon and hurried to Logan who was barely conscious. Ray took his hand and whispered, "If you can hear me, squeeze my hand." Ray felt a very weak squeeze. "We're here; hold on. Oh God, please hold on."

Braxton and Pat lifted Logan onto the mattress, while Logan continued to hold Ray's hand. Pat took the reins and drove the wagon home. About half way there, Ray began to sob as Logan let go of his hand, his arm falling to his side.

Braxton had tears running down his face as he put his arm around Ray's shoulder. Doc Rayburn felt Logan's pulse and listened to his heart. He looked at the others and sadly shook his head and pronounced him dead. Ray's grief was uncontrollable as he sat there covered with Logan's blood. Looking at Logan he said, "Why couldn't you let him shoot me? Why did you step between me and the bullet? Didn't you know that it would have been easier for me to die than to watch you die?"

Ray stared into the distance with a blank look on his face as they rode back to the sheriff's office. When they arrived, Sheriff Ford and Braxton helped Ray off the wagon.

Ford put his arm around Logan's neck and said, "Goodbye, we'll miss you."

"Who did this?" Braxton said. "I want to know who did this."

Ford stared at Braxton with determination in his voice. "We know who did this and we'll deal with them, but right now let's take time to grieve." Braxton nodded. "It was Prescott Monahan's men," Ford said.

Ford told Pat to take the body over to the undertaker. Ray sat on a chair on the walkway and stared blankly into the distance. He would miss Logan the most, the man who was always by his side, anxious to help, no matter how dangerous the job was.

10

The funeral took place the next day. The minister, Shane Banter, held the service and spoke of Logan's faith in Christ. Ray, Sheriff Ford, Pat, and Braxton all said a few words. Then they sang a hymn and the four of them carried Logan's coffin to the grave, lowered it down, and watched as dirt was shoveled in. Braxton couldn't wait to deal with those who were responsible.

Dwight Braxton's two brothers, John and Bob, came riding in as this was going on. The timing couldn't have been better. Dwight introduced his brothers to the others. Ford was rather apprehensive of Braxton's two brothers; old ways were hard to break.

Dwight filled his brothers in on what had happened to Logan, and how they planned to visit Prescott Monahan, a very powerful rancher in Fort Worth. He explained the relationship he had with the others and that he was a deputy of Sheriff Ford. They couldn't hide their amazement. He told them not to be so shocked because he truly wanted to leave his old life behind him and settle down to a respectable life. The three brothers had talked about that but didn't think it was possible.

Brother John spoke first. "Obviously the others must have believed you if they made you a deputy, but it would take a little time for us to adjust to it." Always ready to settle a score, they told Dwight that they would be happy to help in dealing with Monahan and his men.

Sheriff Ford wanted to go to Fort Worth and arrest Prescott Monahan for murder, but he had no jurisdiction in Fort Worth. However the Sheriff of Fort Worth, Chris Weller, was a friend of his and he telegraphed him telling him of his intension.

Sheriff Weller's reply was that Ford had his permission to enter his jurisdiction and arrest Prescott Monahan and any of his men they thought were necessary. He gave Sheriff Ford warning that Monahan would not be easy to take and that he had better come fully prepared. Monahan had about 20 men working for him and that at least three or four of them would be very formidable gunmen. He ended his return telegraph by writing, "Good luck. You're going to need it."

Ford would leave three good deputies behind with Pat to watch the town. He would bring Ray and the three Braxton brothers with him. He couldn't envision any trouble that the five of them wouldn't be able to handle. They wouldn't be gone that long, and the four deputies were fully capable of keeping order in town.

It was a six-hour ride to Fort Worth. When they arrived at the ranch, the five men rode in together to Prescott Monahan's house. There was no doubt in their minds that they could do this. The three Braxton brothers waited outside while Sheriff Ford and Ray went inside and made the arrest. Prescott was surprised to see them. It was a bold move to walk in and arrest him and also a smart move because no one was expecting it.

Ford was firm. Prescott had broken the law in his town, and no one was above the law. They put handcuffs on him at gunpoint and led him out and put him on his horse. They tied his left hand to his saddle horn between his legs, allowing his right hand to hold the reign. He was warned to act like he was riding with them. Dwight Braxton held a hidden gun at his back and said he'd kill him if they were attacked. Prescott was told that he had two choices: ride back to Pleasant Meadows or die on the way.

If anyone started to approach, he was to smile and wave them on. He was furious that he was taken so easily. All of his men were busy doing their jobs and barely noticed. The five men taking him were smiling and talking with him and appeared to be on a casual ride, but they were very intense and ready for quick movement or gunfire.

Prescott made offers of large sums of money for his release. But it was to no effect. Suddenly there seemed to be movement among Prescott's men.

"Wave at them and smile," Ford told Prescott.

"Make one false move and it'll be your last one," Dwight Braxton said. Prescott waved and smiled.

But his men sensed there was something wrong. Six of them rode up behind and started to move around them on both sides. Ford told his men to wait for his signal. He told Dwight Braxton to keep Prescott in sight and shoot him rather than let him get away. Prescott began to sweat profusely.

"Now!" Ford yelled. All five of his men pulled their guns in unison and fired. It was a massacre; all six of Monahan's men went down. The only casualty to Ford's men was a wound in the thigh of Bob Braxton. They made a run for Pleasant Meadows, and no one followed them.

Prescott was locked in a cell while Doc Rayburn tended to Bob Braxton's wound. Ford's men anxiously waited through the night. They didn't know when, but they knew Monahan's men would regroup and come for Prescott at all costs – and they'd better be ready. Logan's death was the last straw. It had changed them into men of war.

Sheriff Ford could not have been happier with the men on his side. He couldn't help but feel good about having four of the fastest guns alive on the side of the law.

The next day ten of Monahan's men rode into town. Dwight, John Braxton, and Ray stood on the walkway facing them, while Sheriff Ford brought Prescott to the door and held a gun to his head. Prescott told them to leave and don't come back until after the trial or he'd be killed.

After a little discussion among themselves, Monahan's men turned around and went back. Ford's men were a little disappointed. They were ready for a war. Monahan would go before the judge in the morning. There was no need to wait. Ford and Ray were the two main witnesses against him, and they wanted to get him out of their jail and off to prison as soon as possible.

In the meantime, James Wakefield had started his training as a Circuit Rider. He was being trained by a circuit rider named John Ashton. Their chosen area was one where few others dared to go and included Indian Territory. Pastor Banter's church was growing and sending out laymen workers who would hold weeklong camp meetings, reaching whole towns with the gospel message.

This, above all, gave Ray's life purpose. He wanted to leave something behind when he was gone, and he felt the end was drawing inevitably closer every day. His study of the Bible made him more and more aware of what was truly important.

His love of God motivated Ray to spend time with the Braxtons each day, as well as the deputies. He witnessed to them about Christ as he went about his daily business. He taught the Indian tribes who would ask him to teach them from what they called "The Holy Book" about the "Great Spirit and His Son." Circumstances made it impossible for him to be a Christian worker like Wakefield, but God enabled Ray to help others in whatever way he could. He knew Ford was praying for him as he tried to help bring law and order to the whole town.

Ray took great comfort in seeing Sheriff Ford

spend time with each prisoner in his jail, no matter what their crimes were, telling them about Christ. He never lost sight of the fact that God loved all men and Christ died for them. No one was beyond His love.

Three days later, the circuit judge came to town, and Monahan's trial was set for the next day. All witnesses were to notified. Monahan's men took seriously Fords warning that Monahan would be killed if his men came back before his trial was over. They stayed away.

Ford wanted to get this trial over with and then, if need be, they would ride back to Fort Worth and settle the score once and for all. In the meantime, they had a town to run. Ford and the businessmen of the town had great plans to make Pleasant Meadows into a thriving town. There was even talk of the railroad coming through Pleasant Meadows. Ray just lived one day at a time, knowing his days were numbered. He had a very simple goal now: do the best he could with the time he had.

The trial was quickly over. The witnesses against Monahan were Sheriff Ford, Ray (using an alias of John Rogers), and Dwight Braxton. Prescott Monahan was sentenced to hang, and it was carried out the next day.

Ford's men did not expect Monahan's men back in Pleasant Meadows. There was no point now, but they would be ready just in case.

The businessmen in town decided it was time to build another hotel and grocery store, and Sheriff Ford realized that the sheriff's office needed to be enlarged. Next door was a hardware store, and he wanted to knock the wall down and enlarge the Sheriff's office; then build a new hardware store across the street. Ford now had eight deputies. As the town grew, the need for more law and order grew with it.

Between his work of spreading the gospel and his work in law enforcement, Ray felt there was purpose for his life. But he knew it could end in a flash at any time, which gave his life a sense of urgency. He wanted to accomplish what God wanted him to do in this life and then go on to the next, rather than have a long earthly life.

Ray had recently lost Amber Marie, who he felt was better never to see again for her sake. And he had lost much more than a friend in Logan Nash. Their absences had left two gaping holes in his life, leaving his world dark and cold. It was his sense of purpose and the knowledge that he would see them again that kept him going.

The upcoming Sunday was what he felt was a milestone in his life. James Wakefield was to preach that morning, and that evening he would answer questions on the reliability of the Bible.

That morning he preached a powerful sermon on Christ's death and resurrection and ended it by saying "Mankind's only hope lay in the lonely hill of Calvary, where the Son of God was crucified for the sin of the world, and rose again and now calls on all mankind to trust in Him for the remission of sin and the new birth from the Holy Spirit."

That evening, one of the questions asked was why Christ had to suffer and die to bring us to God. The answer was that the only way back to God was that His holiness demanded a payment for mankind's sin, one which no man or woman could pay on their own. But God's love for mankind caused Him to come in the Person of Jesus Christ to pay the penalty for our sins and satisfy His Own holiness. This required suffering and death, which also showed the depth and passion of His love for us. Ten people gave their lives to Christ that night, a good omen of what lay ahead for him and his ministry.

That very night a stray dog found by Ray weeks earlier, whom he had named "Baby Girl," gave birth to six puppies that were adopted by the Sheriff's office. Over all, it had been a glorious day.

As the town grew, so too did the possibility for crime. When crime was down, Ford and Ray and the Braxtons carried out the main duties of law and order, while the other deputies helped the people of the town by visiting the sick and shut ins, bringing them medicine and food, and helping with the work on their farms and ranches. Many of the town's people chipped in and helped out with such things as the upkeep on the homes of those not able to do that themselves.

Sheriff Ford, Ray, Dwight and two other deputies, Tom Shore and Greg Treadwell, stayed at the jail and the sheriff's office while the other deputies had rooms across the street at the new hotel. During the night, different men would patrol the streets.

As the town grew, so did the influx of bounty hunters. That wasn't necessarily bad, but in Pleasant Meadows it made Ray nervous. He never knew if they were coming for him. One day there was a downpour of rain as two men were in the street facing each other. One was a bounty hunter, the other a wanted outlaw.

Ray watched from the window of the sheriff's office. The bounty hunter threw the wanted poster at the outlaw's feet. The outlaw spit on it. Both men went for their guns. The bounty hunter was very fast and killed the outlaw. But as Ray watched, another gunman made his way toward the bounty hunter from behind.

Ray moved toward the door as the gunman came up behind the bounty hunter who stood over the man he had just killed. Ray opened the door as the gunman drew his gun, and Ray instantly fired and downed him. The bounty hunter spun around and put another bullet into the gunman.

The bounty hunter turned toward Ray, nodding his head in thanks as he walked toward him. Ray felt very uneasy facing another bounty hunter.

"Thanks," he said, "that man had my number."

Ray went over and checked the body. He was dead. Ray always checked the bodies to see if they were still alive so he could witness to them before they went to meet their Maker.

"Just doing my job," Ray said.

"Maybe so, but I owe you my life." He handed Ray the poster that said the bounty for the outlaw was $500. Ray told him to see sheriff Ford, who was now standing behind him. Ford told him to come on in and have a cup of coffee while they worked things out.

The man came in and sat down. Ray introduced himself as John Rogers. The bounty hunter said his name was John Riddick. Ray brought him a cup of coffee and Ford handed him a receipt book to sign and gave him $500.

Shortly after he left, the stagecoach came into town. It had been robbed and one of the drivers killed. The surviving driver said they were robbed a couple of miles from town. There were four of them. The other driver resisted and he was shot. Two deputies took his body to the coroner's. Ford told Ray and Dwight Braxton to pursue them. If they had robbed the stage a couple of miles away, they couldn't have gone far.

They immediately mounted their horses and rode after them. After five or six miles, they could see them in the distance.

"You're in charge," Dwight said.

Ray shook his head in agreement. "I think we should circle around and come up on them and take them."

"I agree," Dwight said. They rode fast and circled around to a clump of trees and waited.

From behind the trees, they saw when the men came to a place they had been waiting for them to reach. Ray and Dwight rode out into the open and confronted them.

"Throw down your guns; you're under arrest," Ray

yelled. The four men were startled, and for a fleeting moment Ray and Dwight dared to hope they would throw down their guns. But instead they went for their guns.

Ray and Dwight each shot one, and the other two threw their hands up and surrendered. Ray took their gun belts and Dwight reached into his saddlebag and took out some rope and tied one of their wrists to the saddle horn. Then, they rode the ten miles back to town.

They draped the other two bodies on their own horses and headed to town. Ray put the stolen money of $25,000 into his saddlebag. Back in town he turned the money over to Sheriff Ford, who was very surprised that they had captured these men so quickly. Later, Sheriff Ford told pastor Banter that nothing would surprise him that these two men did, and how thankful he was that they were on the side of law and order. The two dead bodies were brought to the coroner and the other two were jailed.

11

The next day was Sunday, and Ray and Ford went to church. A deputy brought Mrs. Fergusson, Sarah Wakefield brought some of her pies, and they all ate them in the Sheriff's office after church. Baby Girl's pups were now big enough to give away. Ray gave one named Misty to Sarah Wakefield, one named Ce-Ce to pastor Banter, one named Spot to Doc Rayburn, and three, Buchaar, Buffy, and Mandy, went to the Sheriff's office. They cheered up the place tremendously.

Things were calm for a stretch after that. Sarah Wakefield's barn was sagging and falling down, and Ray and Dwight thought it a good time to build her a new one before winter. A couple of the deputies and a few people from the town chipped in and helped in their spare time. After six weeks it was finished.

Sarah was very thankful. When she had the time, she helped out at the sheriff's office by cooking and cleaning. Sheriff Ford and the deputies protested that she had more than enough to do with her other jobs plus teaching a large women's Sunday school class and caring for her two children. Many of the women would take her children into their homes while she did her jobs, but she made sure that she spent at least a couple hours every day with them.

Sheriff Ford was greatly respected and even feared by the criminal element because they knew he was backed up by such fierce deputies: Ray Williams and the Braxton brothers. Some of them knew Ray's true identity, and this bothered Ray. Making any future plans was out of the question.

Dwight Braxton had met a girl he was getting serious about, but he had the same problem Ray had. He never knew what his future held. Like Ray, too many folks wanted to see him dead. And like Ray, he wanted out of that life but couldn't see how to do it, and he didn't want to drag her into it.

"I sympathize with you," Ray said. "It's not an easy decision. I know that because I had to do it. But it's one only you can make."

As the town grew. it became harder and harder to collect all the guns as they came into town. Many in town carried their guns. Shootouts in the streets were becoming common.

The Braxton Brothers were notorious for gun battles. John Braxton was confronted by a cocky young man one day who challenged him to a gunfight. "I hear you're fast with a gun. Well I killed 12 men by the time I was twenty," he said.

"So what's your point?" John replied.

"Well my name's Dave Meyer, and I think I'm faster than you." The way he loudly emphasized his name let John know that he was looking for notoriety.

"All right," John said, "You're faster than me. Let's leave it at that!"

Sheriff Ford and Ray overheard and came out of the sheriff's office. "I see you came to save your friend's life!" Dave Meyer said.

"No," Ford said, "We're here to save your life!"

When John Braxton turned to go into the Sheriff's office, the kid pulled his gun and Sheriff Ford slapped it out of his hand and drew his own gun and put the barrel against his nose. "You're under arrest," Ford said.

The kid was humiliated, which was what Ford wanted. Ray led him inside and locked him in a cell. He was clearly shaken.

"You owe the Sheriff your life," Ray said. "Your big mouth almost got you killed. You think gunning people down makes you a big man. Today, John Braxton and the Sheriff showed you real men. Take it to heart and grow up; the graveyard is full of snot-nosed punks like you. You should thank God you're in jail and not the morgue."

In his cell, the snot-nosed punk sat down on the cot with tears running down his face. He hugged his pillow and lay down and cried himself to sleep. He was released the next morning.

Two weeks later, Bob Braxton was ambushed and killed by two men who said that the Braxtons killed their brother and two friends in a gunfight. They shot Bob five times in the back. The Braxton's reputations were catching up with them, and Ray and Dwight were very thankful and relieved that they had both been led to Christ. Ray had the eerie sense that it was only a matter of time until his reputation caught up with him and that time was coming soon.

Bounty hunters were taking no risks and were teaming up to take down men known for fast drawing with a gun and then splitting the reward. And young men were not looking at the long-term effects but only at the immediate effects of a reputation as a fast gun. One thing was clear: the life expectancy of a fast gun was very short. Dwight Braxton accepted that he could never marry and raise a family like other men. His brother Bob's death was a preview of his own.

Pastor Banter conducted the funeral. Ray, Sheriff Ford, Dwight and John Braxton, and the other deputies attended. A number of the town's people attended. It was a solemn time. Pastor Banter said it was "a great comfort, when you bury a person, to know that they knew the

Lord." After the funeral, he gave an invitation to come to Christ. Five people came forward. John Braxton said he knew Bob was looking down and smiling. Then they followed the wagon carrying Bob's coffin to the cemetery and buried him.

Ray could feel the end creeping up on him. It brought him great comfort to see that James Wakefield was persevering in the hard life of a circuit rider and Pastor Banter's work was reaping great results. He was now training laymen to lead camp meetings and to minister to the Indian tribes.

Ray prayed constantly that Amber Marie would marry Bill Eastman and they'd have a good life together, have children, and raise them for Jesus. He wanted to help Sheriff Ford bring law and order to his town. He wanted his life to make a difference for Christ. He had his fill of life and was ready to leave this world.

As they were leaving the cemetery, Dwight and John Braxton were met by gunfire from Dave Meyer who had been released from jail earlier. John was killed and Dwight was wounded before Ford cut Meyer down.

Dwight, who was barely conscious, was rushed to Doc Rayburn's office. Dwight mumbled his concern for his brother John. Sheriff Ford and Ray waited outside in case there were more killers to come. The doctor removed the bullet from between Dwight's left shoulder and collarbone.

Ray dreaded having to tell him that John was dead. He had lost two brothers, and Ray had lost two good friends in a matter of a few days.

That night, Ray stayed in the doctor's office while Ford and two deputies checked around the town for more gunmen. No one slept that night because they were trying to figure out what was going on.

Sheriff Ford was concerned about his law enforcement strategy. He had lost Logan and John and Bob Braxton who, along with Ray Williams and Dwight Braxton, were the solid foundation of law enforcement. Though all were once outlaws, they had a change of heart and were as dedicated to enforcing the law as they had once been breaking the law.

He was thankful he still had Ray and Dwight, but he worried about them. The Braxtons had made a lot of enemies, and their violent past was catching up to them. Ray was different; he was making the most out of the cards that were dealt him. Ray and Braxton had become best of friends and now were inseparable as each watched the other's back.

All the killing had given Ray an idea he wanted to share with Dwight. "How's your lady friend? and by the way, you never did tell me her name."

"Her name's Deborah," Dwight said. "And like you, now more than ever, I know my life could end at any time, and I don't want her hurt."

"But what if you could settle down and get married to Deborah and have a home and children?" Ray asked.

"That would be a great fantasy, but we live in the real world, not a fairy tale where we all live happily ever after," Dwight said.

"Yes, but with careful planning we can create an illusion, a deception for sure, but a good deception. What if when I killed Jack Garth, it wasn't real? What if we faked it?" Ray asked.

Braxton answered quickly. "But it had to be declared a fair fight and the coroner had to sign the death certificate, and don't forget that they buried him."

Ray nodded in agreement. "Yes, that's all true, and don't get me wrong, Jack Garth was definitely dead, but the point is that all the evidence could have been faked."

"Alright, so what are you saying?"

"I'm saying the two of us, me and you, could fake a gunfight where I'd kill you. Sheriff Ford could declare it

a fair fight, our coroner could write out the death certificate, and we could bury an empty coffin. The next thing
you know the newspapers would say you're dead. Then
the wanted posters would be taken down and you'd be forgotten. You could grow a beard and mustache and change
your name. Then, and only then, you and Deborah could
get married with a real wedding.

You could settle down with her, and a few months
later, after you're long forgotten, you can get a job most
anywhere or even work for sheriff Ford under a different
name."

Dwight shook his head. "You've really given this
thing a lot of thought, haven't you? I think maybe it
could work."

When the plan was presented to Sheriff Ford he
was excited about it. "With careful planning we could actually carry it out. We'd have to carry out each step with
great care...and do a heap of praying!"

"What about you? What are you going to do?"
Dwight asked Ray.

"One step at a time," Ray said. "We'll worry about
that when the time comes; right now let's worry about
you."

The first step was to plan out the gunfight. Ray
had to miss Dwight, and they had to make sure no bystanders would get hurt.

After that, the rest seemed pretty easy. The shooting would have to take place near the Sheriff's office.
They wanted a lot of witnesses but no bystanders nearby so all the deputies could quickly surround the body to
keep anyone from seeing no bullet hole or blood. Sheriff
Ford would then pronounce him dead and take him to the
coroner's office.

They planned it for Saturday when there would be
a lot of witnesses. That was five days away. Until then,
Ray and Dwight made it a point not to be seen together.

When Saturday morning dawned, Ray and Sheriff Ford met in Ford's office. Dwight had spent the night in the hotel across the street. They planned for it to take place at noon when there would be a lot of people around in the streets.

At 10 o'clock, Ray walked down to the saloon and asked if Dwight had been in there. The bartender said he hadn't seen him. Ray looked grim. "I have a warrant for his arrest. I'm to bring him in dead or alive."

The bartender shook his head in disbelief. "But he's your best friend."

"I know," Ray said, "but I have my orders and I hope he comes in peacefully. If you see him, tell him I'm looking for him and have a warrant for his arrest. Tell him I want him to turn himself in."

Ray went back to Ford's office and waited on the walkway. The minutes seemed like hours.

About an hour later, Dwight walked down to the sheriff's office as planned. "I hear you're looking for me," Dwight yelled so others could hear him.

Ray stood up, "I have a warrant for your arrest." There were a dozen people at least in the street nearby.

"I guess you'll have to serve it," Dwight said.

Both men went for their guns. Ray fired a shot in the dirt. Braxton went down and lay on the ground. Ford came out of his office with two deputies and knelt down over his body and declared, "He's dead." The deputies put his body on a horse and took him to the coroner's.

By then, the street was filled with people asking what happened. Ray looked down. "I don't want to talk about it." Then he went into the Sheriff's office.

Ford told what was now a crowd that they had received a warrant for Dwight's arrest. Everyone shook their heads in disbelief. Word spread through the town that Ray had killed Dwight Braxton.

That night, Dwight and Deborah took a wagon

about a mile out of town to a cabin where they could work on a new identity. In the meantime, Ray and the deputies would provide anything they needed. Eventually, Dwight could change his identity and name.

News went out over the wire and was picked up by newspapers that the last of the Braxton brothers was dead.

Ray felt in his heart that time was running out for him. He gave $500 to Dwight, $1,000 to James Wakefield, and another $500 to Pastor Banter for his work of ministry.

Next, he began training new deputies for Sheriff Ford. This went on for a couple months. In the meantime, Dwight was secretly changing his identity.

One day Ray rode into town after visiting Dwight Braxton. He dismounted his horse and walked it to the livery stable. In the distance, he could see a Texas Ranger riding in his direction. Inside the stable he spoke a moment with the blacksmith. As he came out, he saw the Ranger dismount his horse and turn and walk toward him. Ray waited with every muscle taut, as the handsome Ranger stopped at a comfortable distance. "You're Ray Williams," he said, not asking a question but stating a fact.

Ray grimly nodded. "I have to take you in," their eyes met, "or try," the Ranger added. In his mind's eye Ray could see what he had seen a thousand times in his fitful dreams, the Ranger going for his gun only to have Ray's bullet rip through his body before his hand ever touched his gun.

"Why don't you just turn around and pretend we never met," Ray said.

"I can't do that," responded the ranger. "I have a job to do.

Ray could see his fingers twitch. The Ranger was clearly nervous, even afraid. "Look son," Ray said, "How you going to take me in when you're lying on the ground with a hole in your chest?"

The Ranger remained silent. Ray desperately wanted to convince him of his folly. Emotion welled up in him, "Son, you're no match for me. I have gone up against the fastest guns alive, and they are all dead. I don't want to add you to the list.

The Ranger clenched his jaw, determined not to let his fears get the best of him.

"Make no mistake about the outcome son; I will kill you."

"I believe you," the Ranger said softly, "but I'm the law and I can't back down."

Ray admired his courage and was reminded of Sheriff Rollins and Sheriff Ford. Ray knew what he had to do. He was done with killing. He breathed a prayer to God, "Lord, I trust in Jesus alone, and I'm ready to come home." A sense of calm came over him like he'd never felt before. His tense muscles relaxed, and he felt a great peace.

"I can't let you take me in son," Ray said, knowing that it would force a confrontation with the ranger.

Then followed a long deadly moment of silence. The bystanders could hear their own hearts beat. Suddenly two guns were drawn but only one was fired. Ray Williams slumped to the ground and fell face down in the dirt. The bystanders were stunned. The ranger walked over to the dying outlaw. He knelt down and gently turned Ray over.

Their eyes met for a moment before Ray's closed. The Ranger could see from Ray's wound that he would not last long. "I'm truly sorry," he said. Ray opened his eyes and nodded, then closed his eyes never to open them again. The turbulent life of Ray Williams was over.

The Ranger's head hung and his shoulders drooped as he walked away. The bystanders solemnly dispersed to their homes. To a man, including the Ranger, all agreed that Ray had drawn his gun before the Ranger's hand ever touched his gun. But he didn't fire and the Ranger did.

The life of Ray Williams was turbulent and full of trials, but God moved his life in the right direction when he heard the gospel message of God's love and grace. It changed his life. And because of that change, what had been a life on a downward spiral ended triumphantly. Though not called to preach, his influence had a great impact on many lives for Christ. James Wakefield reached many people with the gospel as a circuit rider. Pastor Banter reached many more with the gospel of salvation through preparing laymen and sending them out to different towns.

Though this story is fiction it does have a point. Most of us will never do great things for God. We will never split a sea as Moses did, lead God's children into the Promised Land as Joshua did, or win three thousand souls with one sermon as Peter did at Pentecost.

But day by day, trusting God for His commendation alone, and not man's, we can accumulate a lifetime of accomplishments for God. It takes dedication and determination that our lives do have a permanent meaning. Outside of using our lives for Christ, our efforts are like leaving our footprints in the sands of time that the tide will quickly wash away. Only by what we do for Christ can our lives became eternal monuments to God.

Truly it is said: "Only one life twill soon be past, only what's done for Christ will last." It's up to each one of us to decide whether this life is all there is, or if it is a steppingstone to the next life. We must all pray with the psalmist in Psalm 90:12: "So teach us to number our days, that we may apply our hearts to wisdom."

www.ingramcontent.com/pod-product-compliance
Lightning Source LLC
Chambersburg PA
CBHW071536100726
47908CB00004B/1411